ROYAL FLUSH

a pair of plays for preposterous people

John Carney

Key & Candle, Inc.

Published by Key & Candle, Inc.
Jupiter, Florida
keyandcandle.com

ISBN:
978-1-953666-00-0

eBook ISBN:
978-1-953666-01-7

Book design and illustrations by John Carney

To the dead and the deposed.

— JC —

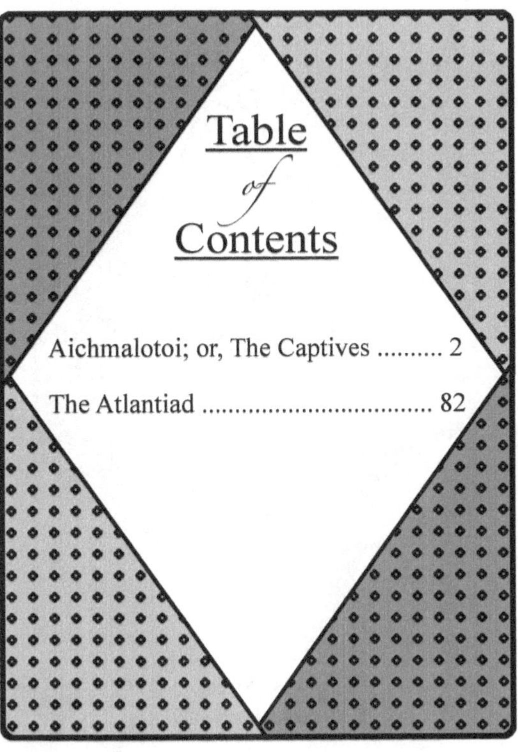

Table *of* Contents

Aichmalotoi; or, The Captives 2

The Atlantiad 82

A

Aichmalotoi; or, The Captives

Dramatis Personae

Marcus Antonius
*Former Triumvir of
Rome*

Cleopatra VII
Pharaoh of Egypt

**Ptolemy XV
'Caesarion'**
*Pharaoh of Egypt, son of
Cleopatra and Caesar*

Alexander Helios
*Son of Cleopatra and
Antonius, twin of Selene*

Selene
*Daughter of Cleopatra
and Antonius, twin of A.
Helios*

Turpio
Slave of Caesarion

Lanuvinus
Slave of Antonius

Timon
Peasant

**Gaius Julius Caesar
Octavianus**
*Imperator of Rome,
former Triumvir*

**Marcus Vipsanius
Agrippa**
*Advisor to Octavian
and General in his
army*

Gaius Cilnius Maecenas
Advisor to Octavian

Octavia Minor
*Sister of Octavian, ex-
wife of Antonius*

**Marcus Aemilius
Lepidus**
*Pontifex Maximus,
former Triumvir of
Rome*

Gaius Sosius
*Former General in
Antonius' army*

Prologue

The curtains remain drawn.
[Enter TURPIO, *center.]*
TURPIO

O, Divine Justice, take heed! I come before you as an emissary from our Poet. He stands faced with that all too familiar accusation: his critics claim that his work has been contaminated by those giants upon whose shoulders he perches. "Give us something new!" they clamor, all the while craving what they know - and what they know, they hate. Therefore, he will take what they know, and make of it something new, and they will hate it all the same. Judge for yourselves then whether our Poet deserves to continue his endeavors or be cast aside - for the same old words from the same old men mean little when weighed against your reception. Thus, I beseech you to pay heed to the pains our Poet has taken. Notice the careful manner in which He uses the characters that you well know to concoct this farce: the prodigal pimp, the greedy whore, the naïve youth, the clever slave, and the braggadocious captain. Our Poet tonight presents you a new production which He has named *Aichmalotoi*; or, The Captives.

The facts stand as such: the two leading men of Rome have been engaged in an intermittent war for fifteen long years. In July of 30 B.C.E., Gaius Julius Caesar Octavianus, soon to be the Emperor Caesar Augustus, arrived in Alexandria to confront Marcus Antonius, soon to be deceased. Antonius had taken up with Caesar's mistress: Cleopatra VII, the great lady of perfection, excellent in counsel, the great one, sacred image of her father, beloved goddess, eminently beautiful and imminently deceased. They had been living in Cleopatra's Palace at Alexandria, and to that same palace the two lovers returned after their fleet was destroyed in the decisive Battle at Actium nearly a year prior to the young Caesar's arrival.

[Exit TURPIO, *center.]*

ACT I

Inside Cleopatra's Palace at Alexandria. Two golden thrones sit on the stage, centered near the rear.
[Enter ANTONIUS, stage right.
He wears Roman military attire
with a sword at his side. He carries
a large, golden cup full of wine.]

ANTONIUS

Ah, Dionysus, your gift gives life! You've always been there for me, waiting with a kiss that's cool in summer and warm in winter, strong in the morning and soft in the evening. Where will you kiss me today?

[Enter CLEOPATRA, stage right.
She wears a yellow dress and
golden jewelry.]

ANTONIUS

There she is, living image of Aphrodite, er, Isis - the goddess taken form anyway-

CLEOPATRA

Is that the Falernian?

ANTONIUS

The wine? Of course it's the Falernian - the elixir of life!

CLEOPATRA

We hardly have any left, and you're spilling it everywhere! Do you have any idea what an amphora costs these days?

ANTONIUS

We have plenty of Falernian left. Just look how full my cup is!

CLEOPATRA

A man should never be allowed to judge his own measures - what you call full nearly always leaves the cup unfulfilled. Anyway, while you've been drinking away the night, Octavian has nearly arrived.

ANTONIUS

Aye, Caesar's other son will be sailing in any moment now.

CLEOPATRA

Caesarion is Caesar's only true son.

ANTONIUS

No, according to Roman law-

CLEOPATRA

I don't favor that word.

ANTONIUS

Roman?

CLEOPATRA

No.

ANTONIUS

What then?

CLEOPATRA

Q No.

ANTONIUS

Q No?

CLEOPATRA

Q No! I don't favor it, and I won't stand for it! Now, what are you going to do?

ANTONIUS

Q Stick to yes, I should think.

CLEOPATRA

Q About the Roman!

ANTONIUS

Q I'm going to keep him out there, and us in here. We can go on for years in here feasting and drinking. My amphorae never run dry.

CLEOPATRA

Q Is that all?

ANTONIUS

Q Well, what are you going to do about him?

CLEOPATRA

Q Maybe we could bribe him.

ANTONIUS

Q Yes, maybe some of your jewels-

CLEOPATRA

Q The slaves. We could sell the slaves and-

ANTONIUS

Q Did you say we could geld the slaves?

CLEOPATRA

Q Geld the slaves? Holy Hathor, not this again-

ANTONIUS

It's brilliant! We'll geld them - all of them, all at once! Fetch my longest sword!

CLEOPATRA

[*Aside*] I'm sure it's not the one you carry.

ANTONIUS

What's that?

CLEOPATRA

Surely not all at once. Anyway, we haven't the time to geld all the slaves. Geld the ones that anger you if you wish - the cook should be able to handle the job easily enough. Then we'll sell them - eunuchs are fetching a good price this week.

ANTONIUS

Yes, tell the cook to geld them, and have him save the trimmings.

CLEOPATRA

There's a fine thought for once. The cook can reprise his recipe for pickled eels. We'll feed them to the remaining slaves and save a bit of the royal grain.

ANTONIUS

You can't feed them to the others - I need those trimmings! I'm going to rain them down on Octavian's head - and just you see if he doesn't try to slip a few inside his toga before he escapes to the rear for a bit of fun with his own.

CLEOPATRA

Gods of Egypt, save me from this drunken idiocy! I don't have any more patience for your nonsense. The Roman will be here soon, and your plans are all cock and no bull! Go on swilling wine then.

[Exit CLEOPATRA, *stage right.]*

ANTONIUS

Swilling wine? I'm embracing my divine role as a priest of Dionysus! Drunk!

[Enter CAESARION, *stage right.]*

ANTONIUS

There he is now, that young son of Caesar. Hail, Little Caesar!

CAESARION

That's not my name! It's Ptolemy XV, heir of the God who saves-

ANTONIUS

Heir of the goat who shaves-

CAESARION

Chosen of Ptah-

ANTONIUS

Chosen of blah-

CAESARION

Son of righteousness-

ANTONIUS

Son of lefteousness-

CAESARION

Address me properly! I'm the Pharaoh of
Upper and-

ANTONIUS

I'll address you with a proper fist about your
head if you keep at it, boy. Your silly Egyptian
names mean nothing to me. I rule here.

CAESARION

Only until I wed.

ANTONIUS

Who would ever marry you?

CAESARION

Mother would.

ANTONIUS

Mother wouldn't.

CAESARION

It's tradition.

ANTONIUS

You're not marrying your mother while I'm
around, Oedipus. You'll have to find another
tradition.

[Enter HELIOS *and* SELENE *from opposite
ends of the stage. They crash into each other
and fall to the ground.]*

ANTONIUS

What's this? Helios, Selene - go play elsewhere, little ones.

[Exit HELIOS *and* SELENE
to opposite ends of the stage.]

ANTONIUS

You're still here? What? What do you want?

CAESARION

I want to know more about Aphrodite.

ANTONIUS

Why?

CAESARION

You said she's your Isis, like mother.

ANTONIUS

Sure, she's our Isis. Anyway, Aphrodite needed a husband, so she interviewed all the Roman gods, from Ares, sacker of cities, to earth-moving Poseidon. All the gods vied for her affection, but she chose for her mate the lame blacksmith, pathetic little Vulcan.

CAESARION

Was he handsome?

ANTONIUS

Ugliest god there ever was.

CAESARION

Was he brave?

ANTONIUS

Complete and total coward.

CAESARION

Was he clever?

ANTONIUS

That much could be said for the decrepit little mutant - he was a bit clever. Clever enough to convince Aphrodite to marry him.

CAESARION

But why would she choose him?

ANTONIUS

Because she knew that with a husband that
weak, she could do whatever she wanted.

CAESARION

And what did she want?

ANTONIUS

She wanted a real man.

CAESARION

So what happened?

ANTONIUS

She married Vulcan, and ran off with Dionysus. Do you remember Dionysus?

CAESARION

The drunk god?

ANTONIUS

The god of wine, boy. He was generous,
jovial, probably the most handsome of all the
gods, definitely the most fun-

CAESARION

But Dionysus can't be the only one she ran off
with.

ANTONIUS

What?

CAESARION

Well, if she would run off with Dionysus, then
she's bound to run off with others.

ANTONIUS

That's not - there's nothing - that is - no more interruptions! You may be the Pharaoh and the heir and the chosen one - you may be the living image of Amun's holy cock - but I rule here. It's only fair - it's my turn, after all. Been my turn since Tarentum, but Octavian stole it from me.

CAESARION

Octavian stole your tarantula?

ANTONIUS

No, idiot, he stole my throne! And he's on his way here now, from Brundisium of all places, on his way to do what he does best - stand himself between Maecenas and Agrippa and squeal like a skewered sow! Caesar he calls himself.

CAESARION

But that's my name!

ANTONIUS

Can you believe the gall of the brat? If he's Caesar, then call me Brutus and Cleopatra Cassius. We will be the new liberators! The brat means to cut short my turn at the helm, but I've still got Roman steel for him to taste - not the taste he takes of his generals' swords, but a proper impaling through the back of his head! And Roman wine for me. The vaults of Alexandria have been well stocked with

Falernian for longer than I've yet lived. Let this new Caesar come then.

[Enter LANUVINUS *and* TURPIO, *stage left.]*

LANUVINUS

Hurry up - follow me. This is the throne room. It's not your place to be in here unless General Antonius calls for you, but he won't. If he needs anything from you, it'll come from me.

TURPIO

What does the general plan to do about the Romans outside the palace?

LANUVINUS

You just worry about watching over Caesarion. General Antonius'll take care of the Romans. And don't interrupt-

ANTONIUS

Lanuvinus, what are you doing? Who's that with you?

LANUVINUS

General Antonius, this is Caesarion's new slave, Turpio - another Egyptian. Palace is barely civilized as it is.

ANTONIUS

A new slave for Little Caesar! What fun. You know, slave, I'm compiling a list for the cook. He's making pickled eels today for a treat, and I bet you could spare a few inches of meat.

TURPIO

Thank you, General, but I have no right to be
included. The quality of my ingredient is so far
inferior to that of your own, and the quantity
too, that it would be an insult to the House of
Ptolemy and the cook. You should have the
place of honor on your list.

LANUVINUS

Don't worry, General - I'll put you at the top
of the list and myself as your number two.
First in rank, first on the list!

ANTONIUS

Stay your hand, halfwit. Why does Caesarion
need a new slave anyway? What happened to
the other one?

CAESARION

He didn't survive your last recipe.

ANTONIUS

No matter - we'll get it right one of these days.
Come with me, Lanuvinus. We will speak with
the cook about his preparations.

[Exit ANTONIUS *and* LANUVINUS, *stage*

right.]

TURPIO

[*Aside*] Did you see the look in the man's
eyes? He won't outfox those Romans. The
drunk god hasn't abandoned him yet, and by
the time he reaches the cook, he won't
remember why he left. I'll have to keep my

time here brief to save my meat and spare your grief.

> *[Enter* HELIOS *and* SELENE *from opposite ends of the stage. They crash into each other, fall to the ground, and exit to opposite ends of the stage.]*

CAESARION

Did you see that, slave? Did you see the two of them?

TURPIO

The two of whom? I see pairs all around me, little Pharaoh.

CAESARION

The twins, stupid! I saw them just now, one on either side, howling as they ran into each other and bouncing back by force of chests - they smote against, and then each wheeled round just there, shouting incomprehensibly. Only look, here they come again!

> *[Enter* HELIOS *and* SELENE *from opposite ends of the stage. They crash into each other and fall to the ground.]*

CAESARION

There, see? That is what I want.

TURPIO

To play with your brother and sister?

> *[Exit* HELIOS *and* SELENE *to opposite*
> *ends of the stage.]*

CAESARION

No, stupid! I want a twin of my own.

TURPIO

Ah, how ignorant of me, but why would you
want such a thing?

CAESARION

Why? How dumb are you? I want a twin so I
have what they have - a constant companion-

TURPIO

Yes.

CAESARION

Someone I can always talk to-

TURPIO

Indeed.

CAESARION

Who would help in any situation-

TURPIO

A true blessing.

CAESARION

Yes, I want a twin.

TURPIO

Of course you do.

CAESARION

Anyway, we Egyptians come in pairs. It's not
just Helios and Selene. Look at Shu and Tefnut
or Geb and Nut. Yes, I will have one of my
own.

TURPIO

But how do you intend to procure this twin?

CAESARION

Money is no object for the Pharaoh of Upper and Lower-

TURPIO

Those Romans are posted right outside the palace doors. You cannot leave safely.

CAESARION

I will not let such a thing prevent my happiness! Those jackals have no authority here! I am the Pharaoh of Upper and Lower Egypt; Ptolemy-

TURPIO

Very well, little master, I will bring you what you seek.

CAESARION

You? How?

TURPIO

I shall have to keep ready for an opportunity and take advantage.

CAESARION

Yes, I suppose you had better. For that is the wish of the Pharaoh of Upper and Lower Egypt; Ptolemy XV Philopater; heir of-

TURPIO

And your wish is my command. Now, go and make your room ready for your new twin.

[Exit CAESARION, *stage right.]*

TURPIO

I can see the beginning of a plot forming, emerging from darkness like the darting rays of Aten's disk cresting over the horizon. Antonius and Cleopatra have sealed their fates, and even the Romans wouldn't do violence to the little ones, but Caesarion is a threat. A Roman Caesar will not want an Egyptian Caesar contending for power, not want to return to Egypt in five years' time to quell another uprising, not want any Roman to remember the bastard son of Caesar. Naïve boy though he is, Caesarion doesn't deserve to die. I'll have to be clever to save the child from the Land of the Dead, while saving the length on my low-hanging head - you all heard what Antonius said!

[Exit TURPIO, *stage left.]*

ACT II

*Outside Cleopatra's Palace at Alexandria.
Octavian's ship is moored stage left, and the mouth
of the bay lies stage right.
[Enter OCTAVIAN, MAECENAS, and
AGRIPPA, stage left. Octavian wears
Roman military attire with a sword at his
side that is so long it drags on the ground
beside him.]*

OCTAVIAN

Alexandria! At last.

MAECENAS

Alexandria.

AGRIPPA

At last.

OCTAVIAN

Let's go in then.

MAECENAS

Steady, Caesar. We've come for diplomacy.

AGRIPPA

Doors are probably locked anyway.

OCTAVIAN

I should offer him single combat and end this farce now.

MAECENAS

There's no need for that. We have him trapped.

OCTAVIAN

I don't want this to be another Mutina, where I graciously let the consuls lead the legions while I bravely oversaw the rear guard. Good thing too because those two got themselves killed! Who knows what would have happened if I hadn't been there to take over.

MAECENAS

Yes, few can match your power in battle, Caesar-

AGRIPPA

And in council you excel all men your age-

MAECENAS

So no one could doubt your strategy-

AGRIPPA

No one! Not in the whole army-

MAECENAS

But you mustn't forget our advice-

AGRIPPA

You must trust in us, Caesar-

MAECENAS

Yes, trust in us - after all, we've been bestow-ed with the benefits of age: wisdom and good sense.

OCTAVIAN

Benefits of age? I'll be thirty-three next month while Agrippa waits for three more months before his birthday! And what of you, Maecenas? A mere five years' difference separates us.

MAECENAS

Yes, Caesar, but together we're over twice your age. None would refuse the advice of one twice their age.

AGRIPPA

Just think what advice you might give a child of fifteen years.

OCTAVIAN

I suppose you're right. Why, even that child of fifteen might guide one of eight, er, seven - well, half-fifteen, anyway. Yes, now I remember your oily words, and their logic still confuses me! There is no surer sign of truth than that - what you say must be so.

MAECENAS

Exactly-

AGRIPPA

Precisely-

MAECENAS

The embassy then-

AGRIPPA

The embassy-

MAECENAS

Great Caesar, since you hold imperium over the whole Roman army-

AGRIPPA

Jupiter himself has chosen you to lead Rome-

MAECENAS

So you must listen to our counsel-

AGRIPPA

No one will offer you a better plan than ours-

MAECENAS

The plan we formed-

AGRIPPA

And still advise-

MAECENAS

Is to send in an embassy-

AGRIPPA

To talk to Antonius-

MAECENAS

To deliver him your terms for his surrender and the surrender of Alexandria-

AGRIPPA

After all, it may take the entire army to storm the palace.

OCTAVIAN

If he won't cede this city, then I'll give him - how many cities are in Egypt?

MAECENAS

Seven, I believe.

OCTAVIAN

Then that's how many I'll burn! I'll give him seven cities burned to the ground! Seven cities such as this, filled with his new people. I'll give him ashes and dust!

MAECENAS

Brave Caesar, send in the embassy first. End
this here and those same cities are yours by
morning.

AGRIPPA

Yes, and what if he should submit to you?

MAECENAS

Come - send the embassy. Old Lepidus first -
Jupiter loves the man, so let him lead the way -
then Gaius Sosius and clever Octavia.

AGRIPPA

I've outfitted her in the disguise of a Centurion
to get her past Cleopatra.

OCTAVIAN

Why don't we just send her in there with a
sword?

AGRIPPA

Shamelessness!

MAECENAS

She goes with the rest under the banner of
truce sanctified by Jupiter himself!

OCTAVIAN

He won't mind.

MAECENAS

You need not bring shame upon yourself over
Antonius. The embassy will do the job.

OCTAVIAN

Oh, very well - send in the embassy.

[Maecenas claps his hands to signal the embassy. Agrippa misunderstands and begins enthusiastically applauding Octavian. Maecenas considers Agrippa; Octavian considers Maecenas; Maecenas realizes he is under inspection and joins Agrippa's applause.]
[Enter OCTAVIA, LEPIDUS, and SOSIUS, stage left. Octavia takes center stage and curtsies in response to the applause.]

OCTAVIAN

Now, let's have a look at each of you. Octavia, dear sister, use your cunning words to move Antonius' heart.

OCTAVIA

Sure you don't want to send me in there with a sword? I'll be certain to move his heart with that.

OCTAVIAN

Shamelessness! You go under the banner of truce sanctified by Jupiter himself!

OCTAVIA

There's no shame in treating a beast as a beast, but I wouldn't kill Antonius. I would just have some fun with him, or make him have some fun with me.

OCTAVIAN

You'll have no sword, but you can tell Antonius that I'll burn the palace down around him if I must. Lepidus, the Egyptian witch might yet surrender - she took flight quickly enough at Actium. After you've each made your case to Antonius, take Cleopatra aside and make her an offer of her own. Let her know that she may survive so long as Antonius does not.

LEPIDUS

And what of her children by Antonius, Caesar?

OCTAVIAN

Tell her what she needs to hear.

LEPIDUS

And what of her child by your uncle, Caesar?

OCTAVIAN

Whatever you like - there's nothing more worthless than promises made to the vanquished. Sosius, that eldest bastard is your responsibility. You've seen the little vulture before - make sure he's still there. I want to end this mess once and for all.

SOSIUS

I remember the look of the boy, Caesar.

OCTAVIAN

Good. Now, go and make ready for your task.

        [Exit OCTAVIAN, MAECENAS,
AGRIPPA, OCTAVIA, LEPIDUS, *and*
        SOSIUS, *stage left.]*

ACT III

Inside Cleopatra's Palace.
[Enter ANTONIUS, CLEOPATRA, *and*
LANUVINUS, *stage right.]*

CLEOPATRA

Is that cup empty again already? I can't tell if you've wasted more through drinking or spilling.

ANTONIUS

Is't spilling or swilling? Anyway, go easy on me. It's hard work I've been doing with the cook. There's a lot of preparation that goes into pickled eels.

CLEOPATRA

Are you still wasting your time worrying about that?

LANUVINUS

It's alright - I've been helping.

[Enter TURPIO, *stage left.]*

CLEOPATRA

So you're both wasting your time on that?

LANUVINUS

No, we-

CLEOPATRA

I don't favor that word! I've heard it enough times today, and I'll not suffer it again!

TURPIO

Lanuvinus, have you just farted?

LANUVINUS

Done what?

TURPIO

Farted. You've farted in the throne room. We all heard it.

CLEOPATRA

Is that true? Have you farted in my throne room?

LANUVINUS

No!

CLEOPATRA

Was I unclear when I told you not to use that word in my presence?

TURPIO

Answer the question, slave! Have you farted?

LANUVINUS

But it was not-

CLEOPATRA

Not is a cousin of no, and I'll host neither today.

LANUVINUS

I mean, my lady, that I believe the sound came from a chair-

TURPIO

You blame your fart on the Pharaoh of Egypt?

LANUVINUS

I-

CLEOPATRA

You.

TURPIO

Which is it then, slave? Have you farted and blamed it on the the Great Lady, Cleopatra?

LANUVINUS

You bend your words like a snake through reeds!

TURPIO

You rend your shorts with a wind in the weave!

CLEOPATRA

Enough, slaves. You, why are you here? What's your business in the throne room?

TURPIO

Masters, and the lesser member of the palace who nevertheless finds himself in the throne room-

LANUVINUS

You insolent-

TURPIO

There is an embassy of Romans at the doors.

ANTONIUS

Romans! Is the coward Octavian with them?

TURPIO

They appear to be two soldiers and a priest.

ANTONIUS

So, two soldiers and a priest walk into the palace in Alexandria. Show them in - let's hear what these Romans have to say.

[Exit TURPIO, *stage left]*

CLEOPATRA

Remember, husband, these are our enemies.

ANTONIUS

Enemies? They're Romans!

[Enter LEPIDUS, SOSIUS, *and* OCTAVIA, *stage left. Octavia is disguised as a Roman soldier.]*

ANTONIUS

Welcome, Romans! Look, wife, dear friends have come our way - my dearest friends in all the world! Lepidus, is that really you? Exile has not been so unkind as the stories we've heard then. Gaius Sosius, have they returned you to me? I have missed you dearly in this land of tricks and deceits. This one I don't recall, but he's a handsome lad. He looks like a true Roman soldier, and he travels in the best company. Cups! Cups for each of my friends!

LANUVINUS

Yes, General. Three cups brimming with wine.

ANTONIUS

Roman wine - the Falernian, elixir of life. And you had better make it four cups - mine is nearly dry.

CLEOPATRA

I'll go. You both mix your wine as though everyday is a feast.

[*Exit* CLEOPATRA *and* LANUVINUS,
stage right.]

OCTAVIA

Your health, Antonius!

ANTONIUS

I like this fellow, but wait for the wine, friend.

OCTAVIA

Hail, Antonius, we all know your amphorae never run dry. We can toast here to our hearts' content, while Octavian, in all his pomp, rages outside. He has vowed to set fire to your city, and make havoc of all the Egyptians in their confusion.

ANTONIUS

You can't trust his vows!

OCTAVIA

And what of your vows?

ANTONIUS

Who is this Centurion? The young man has such a striking look. I'd like to see more of him. Just a peek under the skirt then, eh, lad?

OCTAVIA

Do you not recognize me? You seek a peek between my knees? Will I be recognizable to you from such a view? Come, do my Roman vestments really hide me so well that you

don't see the curve of my hip, my thin arms
and swollen breasts?
ANTONIUS
Who-
OCTAVIA
Oh, husband, how I've missed your touch!
ANTONIUS
Octavia?
OCTAVIA
None other! Now bring me those strong, rough
hands - I want to feel them upon my body
again! Show me how you've missed me, and
I'll wear the bark right off your tree!
[Octavia grabs at Antonius' skirt.]
ANTONIUS
Octavia, control yourself!
OCTAVIA
You're in no place to make demands.
ANTONIUS
Gentlemen, help!
OCTAVIA
Just look at what you've been missing.
[Octavia begins to strip away her disguise.]
ANTONIUS
Stop that! Stop that before-
OCTAVIA
Before what? I need you Antonius, and you
need me. Cleopatra is no match for me
between the sheets!

ANTONIUS

Lepidus, Sosius - deliver me from this lustful woman! Save me from this Bacchanalia!

[Antonius hides behind Lepidus and Sosius.]

OCTAVIA

Very well, Antonius, you're safe for now, but surely your father, Creticus, urged you to set yourself always for the good of Rome. Put aside your quarreling with Octavian. Cede to him, and the Romans old and young will respect you more for doing so. Octavian will make amends if you will. He may even annul our divorce.

ANTONIUS

Royal sister of Octavian, the great betrayer, allow me to say what I have to say. Octavian will never win me over, not for all the wine in the world. No, I've seen before the weight of his promises. Countless cities of men I've stormed and sacked, and from all I took my legal plunder, hauled it away and sent it to Rome. Now, Octavian has seized that same city, Rome, the city that I have suckled with my victories as the she-wolf suckled Romulus!

OCTAVIA

I'll be your she-wolf. Just give me that little Roman sword of yours.

ANTONIUS

Octavian will make no amends now that he has nothing to gain from me, so I will make no pacts with him. Tell him to sail home now.

LEPIDUS

Sail home? Is that what you think he will do?

ANTONIUS

Well, it's quite a long walk.

LEPIDUS

Your judgement has been overpowered by some force. Look at me, Antonius. Aged though I am, I was your colleague too. Take me as your example, and cede now to Octavian. Don't suffer as I did at Sicily.

ANTONIUS

What happened at Sicily?

LEPIDUS

You ate an apple suspiciously?

ANTONIUS

You said you suffered at Sicily.

LEPIDUS

I did! When I put down that revolt led by Pompey's son. I defeated those traitors, with my legions at my back. Octavian asked me to step down then, to take my legions back. He offered me rewards for my victory - a good share of the plunder taken from Sextus Pompey and a place of honor in his Ovation. I wouldn't have it. I wanted the Ovation for myself. At the least, he could have named me as his partner-in-arms and shared the Ovation.

ANTONIUS

Lepidus, old friend, you won those battles- those lands were yours by right, as was the Ovation! Octavian should have done the honorable thing and hailed you in your triumph. And what about your legions?

LEPIDUS

I don't have any lesions, Antonius, but my plug has sprung a leak in old age - I've already dribbled all over your stage!

ANTONIUS

The men, Lepidus.

LEPIDUS

The men were behind me all the way! Just until they defected to Octavian. Then I had my just rewards-

ANTONIUS

You had ostracization!

LEPIDUS

No, I've never been to Ostrich Nation. No, Antonius, I had to fall on my knees and beg of Octavian that which he now offers you - exile, a life of sober solitude.

ANTONIUS

Ah, Lepidus, my old, old friend, you should not have stepped down at Sicily.

LEPIDUS

And you, glorious General Antonius, you have earned your rest, paid for it in blood across this vast empire. Fire this war anew, and your flame will flag, and no longer will Romans honor you.

ANTONIUS

I say my honor lies here, in the kingdom of Egypt. Another thing - it degrades you to serve Octavian's pleasure, that cowardly son of Caesar! It would do you proud to stand by me now.

LEPIDUS

How can I stand by a minnow? Swim perhaps.

ANTONIUS

I said-

SOSIUS

Ready, friends? Come, away we go now. There's no achieving our mission here. Best to return to Octavian and give our report at once - Antonius will not yield. He will not pay the price for this truce that his friends so desire. The gods have planted a fury in your chest, Antonius - they have made you cruel and relentless, and all for a title. Show respect for your own city! Here we are, sent from Rome, your closest, dearest friends. We long for you to set aside your grievances and make peace with Octavian.

ANTONIUS

Gaius Sosius, general of my armies, well said. But my heart still burns with anger and hatred whenever I remember his arrogance - and also when I eat the little black olives stuffed with garlic. But Octavian, he usurped me before all of Rome! That ersatz son of Caesar treated me like some outcast. You go back to him and relay my message - he'll not take this palace while I yet draw breath. I'll defend it to the hilt!

OCTAVIA

You can rear-end me to the hilt!

[Enter CAESARION, *stage right.]*

CAESARION

What's this? Ambassadors from Rome? Why was I not summoned?

ANTONIUS

Now you're all in for an earful. You should have left when Sosius suggested it.

LEPIDUS

Caesarion, is that you?

CAESARION

Who's this old man?

LEPIDUS

My name is Marcus Aemilius Lepidus.

CAESARION

What do you want, old man Lepidus?

LEPIDUS

I was a friend of your father. Do you not recognize me, child?

CAESARION

I do not, and you may address me as Pharaoh Ptolemy XV.

ANTONIUS

You see what I mean?

> *[Enter* CLEOPATRA *and* LANUVINUS, *stage right. Lanuvinus bears four cups. He distributes them to the embassy and Antonius.]*

LANUVINUS

Cups! Four cups of the best wine that-

ANTONIUS

What took you so long?

LANUVINUS

We would have been back sooner, but the great lady made me add more water four times! An eel could live in each of those cups.

CLEOPATRA

You're mistaken, slave. Eels don't belong in cups - they get pickled in the kitchen. And I know just where to find an extra one, shriveled and peculiar though it may be.

ANTONIUS

You'd better get moving, Lanuvinus, before she takes your little penis.

> *[Exit* LANUVINUS, *stage right.]*

*[The six remaining actors split into pairs:
Octavia and Antonius, stage right;
Cleopatra and Lepidus, center; and
Caesarion and Sosius, stage left.]*

OCTAVIA

Antonius, speak with me.

ANTONIUS

You need to go! Put this uniform back on before Cleopatra realizes who you are.

OCTAVIA

You should really be worrying about yourself. I'm maybe the only person in the world who could keep my brother from killing you. I could persuade him to let you live. That is, I could persuade him to let my husband live. Just promise to give me what you have under those skirts every night. I need you, Antonius! I want to feel you in my-

LEPIDUS

But, Cleopatra, think of your children.

CLEOPATRA

What about them?

LEPIDUS

Caesar has mercy to match his generosity. He is willing to let them live if you help him end this siege.

CLEOPATRA

At what price? I'll not be held to ransom.

LEPIDUS

He is willing to let you keep your ransoms.

CLEOPATRA

No ransom? I keep my gold, my jewels?

LEPIDUS

You may keep your gold, your jewels, whatever you like. What need has Caesar of any of
this? As long as you continue to pay tribute to
Rome, you will keep it all.

CLEOPATRA

Can the new Caesar be trusted?

LEPIDUS

He can be trusted to-

SOSIUS

Twist my auger! It's Little Caesar!

CAESARION

Address me properly, soldier.

SOSIUS

Look at that - same Little Caesar.

CAESARION

That's not my name!

SOSIUS

Just the same. How are you, Little Caesar?

CAESARION

I'm not Little Caesar! I'm the Pharaoh of
Egypt!

SOSIUS

But Romans have no Pharaoh, so you are
nothing to me, nobody.

CAESARION

Am too!

SOSIUS

Are not, Little Caesar Nobody.

CAESARION

Say that again and-

CLEOPATRA

I'll yield. What does he ask of me?

LEPIDUS

Remarkably little, Pharaoh. Caesar asks only
that you keep Antonius' cup filled and the
doors unlocked. Do this and he will guarantee
your throne with just rewards as well.

CLEOPATRA

Antonius' amphorae never run dry - and my
purse is never full - but to be the Egyptian
Sinon?

LEPIDUS

Were your ancestors not themselves Greek?

CLEOPATRA

Not the type of Greeks to turn their city over
to some-

ANTONIUS

Sex-crazed woman! Stop it! Stop it, I said!
That's an order!

OCTAVIA

That's not the type of order I'll take from you!
Now, report to the bedroom and assume the
position!

ANTONIUS

I am a Roman General!

OCTAVIA

You're no Roman, and I'm no soldier. You'll just have to make me obey, husband.

ANTONIUS

[*to all*] Enough! I've heard enough - Octavian won't win me over. Now, out with you!

SOSIUS

Remember what we have said, General Antonius.

LEPIDUS

And you, Cleopatra. Farewell, Antonius.

ANTONIUS

Farewell, Romans.

OCTAVIA

Farewell, Egyptians.

SOSIUS

Bye-bye, Little Caesar Nobody!

    [Exit OCTAVIA, LEPIDUS, *and* SOSIUS,

                        stage left.]

CLEOPATRA

So, two soldiers and a priest walk out of the palace in Alexandria. Well, what now?

ANTONIUS

What now?

CLEOPATRA

When will you surrender?

ANTONIUS

Surrender? Why would we surrender?

CLEOPATRA

You heard what the Romans said! What if they burn down the palace?

ANTONIUS

Then we won't have to surrender.

CLEOPATRA

You act cavalierly enough with your own life, but you would waste mine too?

ANTONIUS

You would cling so greedily to life as to suffer the shame of surrender?

CAESARION

Never mind that - who was that Roman you were talking to?

ANTONIUS

Just another Roman.

CLEOPATRA

Not just another Roman - a Roman soldier. What did he want?

ANTONIUS

To remember past engagements. What about Lepidus? What did he have to say?

CLEOPATRA

Nothing. Just that Octavian is a liar.

ANTONIUS

And a coward!

CLEOPATRA

We can't trust anything that comes from that one.

ANTONIUS

What about Sosius? I miss that man around here. What did he have to say?

CAESARION

Sosius is a brute! He called me Little Caesar Nobody! I want him killed.

ANTONIUS

Do you? Here's my sword-

CLEOPATRA

[*Aside*] Fitted perfectly for a child's hand.

ANTONIUS

Sosius is just outside now. Go and kill him.

CAESARION

The Pharaoh does not take care of such things for himself!

ANTONIUS

A Roman does.

CLEOPATRA

A Roman takes care of all manner of things for himself.

ANTONIUS

And an Egyptian cares for herself above all else.

[*Exit* CLEOPATRA, *followed by*
ANTONIUS, *stage right.]*

CAESARION

> What do I care what a Roman does? Anyway, I have slaves for such things.
>
> *[Enter* TURPIO, *stage left. He collects Octavia's vestments.]*

TURPIO

> What's all this? A discarded disguise to aid my endeavor?

CAESARION

> You! Where have you been?

TURPIO

> Waiting to serve - it's the greatest pleasure in my life. Where did all this come from?

CAESARION

> The usurper, Octavian, sent his underlings in to try to scare us off. Now, where's my twin?

TURPIO

> Patience, young master. I will bring you what you need.

CAESARION

> You'd better! Because I heard Antonius say the cook is making something special for dinner tonight - pickled eels from a secret recipe! If you don't get my twin, then you can't have any.

TURPIO

> It would be a shame to miss such a delectable dish.
>
> *[Exit* CAESARION, *stage right.]*

TURPIO

Great gods of Egypt, Aten has finally risen - I
see the light! Caesarion's twin will be his
escape. I'll slip into town for a matching
jackanapes. 'Tis better to stay away for now as
well, lest Antonius should make good on his
japes and take away all the length that hangs
past my grapes!

[*Exit* TURPIO, *stage left.*]

ACT IV

Outside Cleopatra's Palace.
[Enter OCTAVIA, LEPIDUS, *and* SOSIUS,
center.]

SOSIUS

That was him alright - arrogant little pyramid
builder.

LEPIDUS

That's the son of deified Caesar.

SOSIUS

His son by Cleopatra, the witch of Egypt.
Anyway, new Caesar says the boy's a demon.

LEPIDUS

Nonsense. He just needs a bit of learning.

SOSIUS

He needs a bit of caning.

OCTAVIA

I know what Antonius needs! Everyone could
see it.

SOSIUS

I've never seen General Antonius so angry. I
thought his head was going to explode.

OCTAVIA

I'll make his head explode alright.

LEPIDUS

Enough, woman! Antonius doesn't want you.

OCTAVIA

How can you say that? Of course he wants me!

SOSIUS

You're lucky you didn't ruin the whole thing, Pasiphaë!

[Enter MAECENAS *and* AGRIPPA, *stage left.]*

MAECENAS

At last! How did it go, friends?

OCTAVIA

Poorly.

AGRIPPA

Octavia, what happened to your disguise?

OCTAVIA

I had to show Antonius the Roman hills he's been missing, and he would have succumbed to me if these two had only let me get my hands on him!

MAECENAS

Dear lady, what if Cleopatra had recognized you? She would have had you executed on the spot.

OCTAVIA

Antonius would never have let her do such a thing. The man is still mad for me.

LEPIDUS

Cleopatra was far too distracted by Caesar's offer to take any notice of Octavia's antics.

AGRIPPA

She accepted then? She'll end it?

LEPIDUS

Yes, at daybreak tomorrow.

MAECENAS

Then the end of this farce is near, and Rome awaits our return. We'll fetch Caesar now, and share the good news! Come, Agrippa

AGRIPPA

To Caesar!

> *[Exit* MAECENAS *and* AGRIPPA, *stage left.]*

LEPIDUS

Ah, but, Maecenas, the farce is never ending. Fortune never tires of interfering with human affairs. Low men are brought hight, high men are brought low. Finally, we all end in a shallow furrow.

OCTAVIA

I'd let Antonius end in my furrow.

> *[Enter* OCTAVIAN, *stage left.]*

OCTAVIAN

Well? What happened? Tell me, dear sister, pride of Rome - will he save the palace from burning, or did he refuse? Is he coming out?

OCTAVIA

Most noble son of Caesar, Antonius will not come! He spurned me and my gifts, and bade you to sail home.

OCTAVIAN

The most wasteful scoundrel in all of Rome! And Cleopatra? What did she say?

LEPIDUS

The lady Cleopatra was amenable to your overture.

OCTAVIAN

Huh?

LEPIDUS

She affirmed your proposition.

OCTAVIAN

Speak sense, old man!

LEPIDUS

She said yes.

OCTAVIAN

Then the drunken fiend is mine! I will tell Agrippa to ready the cohort.

LEPIDUS

Steady, Caesar - you must be patient. The lady stated your terms will be met by sunset.

OCTAVIAN

Why not now? Who knows what kind of schedule these Egyptians keep their sun on.

LEPIDUS

It will take quite a bit more wine to subdue Antonius. Give the man some time to drink his last cups.

OCTAVIAN

Very well. What of the demon, Sosius, was it there?

SOSIUS

Aye, he was there.

OCTAVIAN

And?

SOSIUS

And...

OCTAVIAN

Did it have scales? How long was its tail? How many horns did it have?

SOSIUS

No scales, Caesar, nor tail nor horns that I saw.

OCTAVIAN

The little imp must have been hiding it all. These Egyptians do marvelous things with their makeup. It doesn't matter. The creature is already as good as dead! I want you to deal with it when the time comes, Sosius.

SOSIUS

Aye, Caesar.

OCTAVIAN

Yes, you, Sosius. Now, you may await my return to the ship.

[Exit OCTAVIA, LEPIDUS, *and* SOSIUS,

stage left.]

[Enter TURPIO, *center. He wears Octavia's discarded disguise.]*

OCTAVIAN

Where'd you come from, soldier?

TURPIO

From the palace, sir.

OCTAVIAN

What were you doing in the palace?

TURPIO

Caesar commanded it, sir.

OCTAVIAN

I commanded? I sent only three inside!

TURPIO

Yes, sir, er, Caesar, three went into the palace, while you remained here as the fourth.

OCTAVIAN

With Maecenas and Agrippa - don't forget them.

TURPIO

Right, three went into the palace, while you remained here as the fourth, with Maecenas and Agrippa making five and six.

OCTAVIAN

But they only count as one.

TURPIO

One?

OCTAVIAN

One.

TURPIO

How one?

OCTAVIAN

They combined their ages, see, so it's just the one of them.

TURPIO

Right, so three went into the palace, while you remained here as the fourth, with Maecenas and Agrippa making five. But if Maecenas and Agrippa are each less than one person, then it stands to reason that neither should be counted, for how can you count a person as whole who is half? So four is the number.

OCTAVIAN

Four! That's right!

TURPIO

And four have exited the palace - Octavia, Lepidus, Sosius, and a soldier whose name does not bear mentioning - while you have remained here with Maecenas and Agrippa, none of whom should be counted.

OCTAVIAN

Well, four have exited, and I have remained here... Carry on then, soldier!

[Exit OCTAVIAN, *stage left.]*

TURPIO

This Caesar's more stupid than I had im-agined, but he's found an apt rival in Antonius inebriated and impassioned. Now a fool and a drunk hold the city at bay, but who'll write that truth of this silly play? Though I trust

you'll remember what you saw here today
whenever you see a straw man burned away.
[Exit TURPIO, stage right.]

ACT V

Inside Cleopatra's Palace.
[Enter CLEOPATRA, *stage right.]*

CLEOPATRA

    I suppose there's no chance of escape now - no simple ruse will fool those soldiers outside. I'll have to do as Lepidus bids me and take Octavian's offer. How else can I keep my palace, my gold, my jewels? This is the very history of Egypt, and only I am Egyptian enough to keep it all. Antonius is doomed anyway - why should I waste everything for him?

    [Cleopatra unlocks the door to the throne room.]

CLEOPATRA

    That's twice now I've rendered Egypt unto Caesar.

    [Enter ANTONIUS *and* LANUVINUS, *stage right.]*

ANTONIUS

    Cleopatra, my beauty, is it time for bed?

CLEOPATRA

    It is for me, but I fear something will keep you away from me all night.

ANTONIUS

    What?

CLEOPATRA

I don't particularly care, so long as it is effective.

ANTONIUS

Do you ever tire of your games?

CLEOPATRA

Do you ever tire of your shames?

ANTONIUS

What's this? Insults from a Greek pretending to be an Egyptian?

CLEOPATRA

Better than a Roman who thinks he's Greek pretending to be an Egyptian!

ANTONIUS

That's right - Roman to the hilt!

CLEOPATRA

The blade hasn't got far to go if it's your sword!

ANTONIUS

The Roman sword is a soldier's prize!

CLEOPATRA

Pity it isn't known for its size! And if you're so Roman, why are you fighting against Rome? You should surrender now, and save yourself some humiliation!

[Exit CLEOPATRA, *stage right.]*

ANTONIUS

Come, Lanuvinus - there are decisions to be made tonight. Cleopatra would have me

surrender the palace and fall on Roman mercy,
but I've never known Octavian to be merciful.

LANUVINUS

Perhaps the boy has developed mercy with
age.

ANTONIUS

And perhaps a porcupine will develop
feathers, a seagull will develop a trunk, and
you will develop a new cock when the cook
hacks yours off! No, only one thing is sure to
develop with age - go and fetch me some more
of the Falernian.

LANUVINUS

Yes, master. A cup of Falernian.

ANTONIUS

Better make it a bowl. It's going to be a long
night.

[Exit LANUVINUS, *stage left.]*

ANTONIUS

What I do now, I do for the good of all of
Rome. I must fight on. I must ensure that this
scheming coward doesn't destroy everything
that I have helped to build here and in Rome.
No, I'll not surrender, and we can hold out
here for months, years maybe.

[Enter LANUVINUS, *stage left.]*

LANUVINUS

There's none left, General.

ANTONIUS

Of course there is.

LANUVINUS

It appears there isn't, master.

ANTONIUS

No, there must be more down there. I've never run out before. Go and take another look, and if you can't find some more, then report to the cook!

LANUVINUS

Away with me then to search every nook!

ANTONIUS

Rest easy, Lanuvinus, I'll forfeit my life before I let these Egyptians take a sword from a Roman, even a little paring knife from a slave like yourself.

LANUVINUS

Master Antonius, regretfully I must report that there is not a drop of Falernian left in all the storerooms.

ANTONIUS

Do you mean to tell me that this is the end? The last cup of Falernian in the palace?

LANUVINUS

General, your amphorae have run dry.

ANTONIUS

Abandoned by Dionysus. Very well, I know what I must do.

[Antonius draws his sword from his scabbard with a flourish. It's length is underwhelming - it's clear that the blade filled less than half the scabbard's length.]

LANUVINUS

Master, no!

[Antonius stabs himself in the chest.]

LANUVINUS

Antonius, what have you done?

ANTONIUS

Go and tell the coward he will find the King of Egypt in the throne room.

[Antonius dies.]

LANUVINUS

Antonius, son of Rome, I'll see that Charon gets his due. Oh, you stab so deep you hit my own heart too! For what now of me? What of the last Roman in Cleopatra's Palace? Maybe if I let in those Roman soldiers outside, then they would let me return home with them. They'll know a Roman when they see one, and we're all brothers again now that Antonius is dead. Better to try my luck with them than stay with Cleopatra. She'll have my head once she sees Antonius dead - although, at least she's only after one of my heads. She would never

waste a slave with such games as Antonius.
Yes, at least I'm safe from the cook. Hey,
that's right! My tip won't be clipped! My cock
is safe from the cook's chopping block! My
dangling container is no longer endangered!
[Enter TURPIO *and* TIMON, *center. Turpio
still wears Octavia's Centurion disguise.
Timon resembles Caesarion, but the former
is a full head shorter than the latter.]*

LANUVINUS

Who's that? Praise Jupiter, a fellow Roman!
Look here, General Antonius is dead.

TURPIO

Antonius dead? Osiris beware - a trickster is in
your midst. This one's not as clever as Set, but
keep a close eye on Isis and Nepthys.

LANUVINUS

Osiris, Set, Isis, Nepthys? That's no Roman -
Turpio? What are you doing in those soldier's
clothes?

TURPIO

Never mind that - Antonius is dead! How did
he die?

LANUVINUS

He fell on his sword - an honorable Roman
death for an honorable Roman warrior.

TURPIO

You Romans are a bit funny - shouldn't a
warrior fall in battle?

LANUVINUS

What do you know of Rome?

TURPIO

I know that the death of a general is a solemn
occasion.

LANUVINUS

That's true, at least.

TURPIO

And I know that words are traditionally said
over the body of the deceased.

LANUVINUS

Aye, fancy-type words, but I'm not one who
knows such.

TURPIO

I know some appropriate words to say for
somber occasions.

LANUVINUS

You'd do that for General Antonius?

TURPIO

No, Lanuvinus, I'd do it for you.

LANUVINUS

Thank you, Turpio. Maybe not all Egyptians
are uneducated, uncivilized simpletons.

TURPIO

So a man walks into the library at Alexandria
and asks the librarian for a scroll about
suicide.

LANUVINUS

This is no time for jokes!

TURPIO

You're supposed to ask what the librarian said.

LANUVINUS

I don't care what the librarian said!

TURPIO

No, dummy, she calls back - Fuck off! You won't return it.

LANUVINUS

I already told you, this is no time for jokes!

TURPIO

It's always time for jokes. What is life but a joke to which you never learn the punchline?

LANUVINUS

Where'd you hear such nonsense?

TURPIO

Timon told me.

LANUVINUS

Who's Timon?

TIMON

I'm Timon.

LANUVINUS

Who's that?

TURPIO

That's Timon.

LANUVINUS

Who's Timon?

TURPIO

He's a misanthropist.

LANUVINUS

A misanthra-what?

[Enter CAESARION, *stage right.]*

CAESARION

Who's that?

TURPIO

That's Timon.

CAESARION

Who's Timon?

LANUVINUS

Don't go near him, young master! He's a rapist
from Misanth!

TURPIO

This is your twin.

CAESARION

My twin?

LANUVINUS

Caesarion has a twin from Misanth?

CAESARION

This is not my twin.

TURPIO

Not yet.

CAESARION

Not ever! He's supposed to be a girl, stupid!

TURPIO

A girl? Not all twins are like your brother and
sister.

CAESARION

This is all wrong! It's supposed to be a girl!

TURPIO

Look, this is the twin I've found you. What's
wrong with him anyway?

CAESARION

I told you - I want a twin like Helios and Selene, like Geb and Nut. A twin to wed, stupid! I
can't very well wed a man!

TURPIO

Perhaps you could. Just give him a chance -
you might like him.

CAESARION

Like him? What's to like?

TURPIO

What's to like? Look at him! He looks just like
you!

CAESARION

He doesn't look like me! With those dirty
hands and suntanned arms? Wearing those rags
that scarcely cover his broad shoulders and
strong chest? That rich crown of hair and those
kind eyes; that heroic brow and perfect nose;
those soft lips, gentle hips, and fine legs.

TURPIO

Indeed, what's to like about any of that? I'll
remove him from the palace immediately.

CAESARION

Don't be hasty.

TURPIO

No, no - you're right. I've gotten it all wrong, and this one won't do.

CAESARION

Well, look, I suppose you have already found him. Where did you find him anyway?

TURPIO

I bought him from a slaver near the Timonium.

TIMON

And him no worse for the transaction. Men are made of the very filth that they float down the Nile - excrement borne of excrement.

CAESARION

Does he smile.

TIMON

He does not.

TURPIO

But he won't become your twin until you give me your word that you will follow my commands.

LANUVINUS

You? Command the Pharaoh?

TURPIO

It is the only way that I will release Timon from his bond to me.

TIMON

Bound to men, bound to life - but which of the two is the worse?

CAESARION

And why should I want a slave for a twin?

TURPIO

He won't be a slave any longer once he be-
comes your twin, and then you will have what
you need.

CAESARION

Well - alright.

TURPIO

Your word, young master.

CAESARION

I give you my word as Ptolemy XV
Philopater-

TURPIO

Save the rest - we're a bit short on time. And,
to really make him feel like your twin, give
Timon your jewels.

CAESARION

What?

TURPIO

You gave me your word, and twins share.

CAESARION

Oh, very well!

TURPIO

Now, something more valuable still.

CAESARION

More valuable than all my gold?

TURPIO

He needs your name. Timon, you are now
Caesarion - Caesarion, you are now Timon.

TIMON

It's a sorrow to meet you. I hope the name
does you no good, just as it did me.

CAESARION

Oh, well, I hope you like your name. There's
more to it than that though. Caesarion is just
my short name. My full name is-

TURPIO

You mean his full name.

CAESARION

You know what I mean! Anyway, it's Ptolemy
XV Philopater; heir of the-

TIMON

That's too many names for me.

TURPIO

You can't very well be Timon any longer.

CAESARION

Why can't he?

TURPIO

Because that name is yours now.

CAESARION

He could have it back. I don't mind.

TURPIO

Don't be ridiculous - you can't just go trading
names as you like.

CAESARION

But-

TIMON

What use have I of a name? Death lies in wait for all men around any corner, and my name will not be remembered. Even if my name should live on in inscriptions, I will not. Call me 'Nobody' and be done with it.

[Enter OCTAVIAN *and* SOSIUS, *center.]*

OCTAVIAN

Victory is mine! By my own sheer force of strength, I have defeated the whole of Antonius' armies. Come out here, you shameful drunk, so I can accept your surrender!

LANUVINUS

As I've been saying, Antonius is dead.

OCTAVIAN

Antonius dead? Sosius, check the body.

SOSIUS

Aye.

OCTAVIAN

You.

SOSIUS

No, 'aye' means 'yes.'

OCTAVIAN

That's poor conjugating, Sosius. You should say, 'I mean yes.'

SOSIUS

I mean, it's him, Caesar. He's the general.
General Antonius, that is. Not me.

OCTAVIAN

And? Is he dead?

SOSIUS

Dead drunk by the smell of him! I've seen him
like this afore - he can really put away his
wine, Antonius can. Come on, General - up
you get!

    *[Sosius stands astride Antonius and heaves
    his body up.]*

SOSIUS

The general appears to be leaking, Caesar.
Might be he spilled his wine.

LANUVINUS

It's his blood, you fool!

    *[Lanuvinus puts his hand to the ground, then
    brings it to his mouth.]*

LANUVINUS

His blood tastes like his piss.

TURPIO

[to Lanuvinus] Can't you see the man is dead?

LANUVINUS

[to Sosius] Yeah, can't you see the man is
dead?

    [Sosius roughly drops Antonius' body.]

SOSIUS

Who's this one then?

TURPIO

Looks like one of the Egyptian palace slaves.

LANUVINUS

You filthy liar! I'm a Roman-

SOSIUS

Enough of that! You're profaning afore the highest man in all Rome.

OCTAVIAN

What do we do with him?

TURPIO

Send him to the kitchen. The cook will know what to do with him.

LANUVINUS

My cock!

[Sosius punches Lanuvinus in the stomach.]

SOSIUS

What did I tell you? No more talking from you, or I'll slice that tongue right out of your head.

OCTAVIAN

And this one? Who is he?

TIMON

I'm not anyone - I'm Nobody.

SOSIUS

That's Little Caesar! Just look at his jewels.

TIMON

That's not my name.

SOSIUS

That's him alright!

71

TURPIO

You should address him properly - that's
Ptolemy XV Philopater, heir of the god who
saves, chosen of Ptah, sun of righteousness,
living image of Amun, the young Caesarion.

OCTAVIAN

Young Ptolemy, you die today!

TIMON

Don't do me any favors.

OCTAVIAN

Favors? I'll do you no damn favors, boy! I'm
going to have you killed!

TIMON

Such a kind man to spare me a life of misery
and disappointment.

OCTAVIAN

I'll spare you nothing! You'll suffer misery
and disappointment when Sosius takes your
head! The man is practiced. And all the worse
for you since he used to serve this very house.
You should never have crossed the great-

TIMON

Look, if I'm to die, let's hurry it along a bit. If
you think of anything else clever to say, just
tell everyone you said it.

OCTAVIAN

Get them out of my sight, Sosius!

LANUVINUS

Turpio, help!

OCTAVIAN

Who's Turpio?

TURPIO

Must be one of their Egyptian gods - they have such strange names down here.

OCTAVIAN

What about this one?

TURPIO

Looks like another slave, Caesar.

OCTAVIAN

Another slave? How many is that?

TURPIO

It's-

OCTAVIAN

I know how to count! There was one, then two, then... What comes after two?

TURPIO

What?

OCTAVIAN

Right, what. There was one, two, what... What comes after what?

TURPIO

A question mark?

OCTAVIAN

Right, one, two, what, question mark - how many is that?

TURPIO

Too many, Caesar. I'll set him loose on the mainland.

OCTAVIAN

Yes, go, child, and tell all of your little Egyptian friends of Caesar's mercy to freemen. Now, get him out of here, so I can murder the demon.

[Exit TURPIO *and* CAESARION, *center.]*

OCTAVIAN

Victory! It's true what they say - victory is all the sweeter when it's won on the battlefield. Antonius, well, he only killed himself for fear of me, so that's even better than defeating him in combat. And the boy, I can still kill the boy. We can have a battle too - I'll even give him a sword...well, maybe a knife. Sosius!

[Enter SOSIUS, *stage left.]*

SOSIUS

Caesar?

OCTAVIAN

The boy, bring me the boy.

SOSIUS

It's already done, Caesar.

OCTAVIAN

The boy is dead then?

SOSIUS

Aye, I killed him myself.

OCTAVIAN

Yes, you-you killed him but at my command.

SOSIUS

Caesar?

OCTAVIAN

You-you killed him at my command, so it's rather more like I killed him, wouldn't you-you say?

SOSIUS

Would I?

OCTAVIAN

You would. Just as I thought. So if anyone asks, I killed the boy. And he had a knife. No! A sword - bigger than mine even. Well, no, not bigger than mine. He attacked me with a sword that was almost as big as my own, but I killed him.

SOSIUS

As you say, Caesar. No stranger than what the cook wanted to do with him.

OCTAVIAN

What do you mean?

SOSIUS

Well, he had the other one, the slave, he had him walk right up to the table, remove his little bald man from his tunic, and set it right across the table in front of him. Then he brought out the biggest knife I've ever seen in my whole life. Bit mean pulling out a knife that big for a thing that small. Anyway, his hand dropped with a chop, and the little thing fell off! But I don't think he was very practiced because the slave is bleeding everywhere. What should I do with him?

OCTAVIAN

What do I care if some Egyptian lost his staff? The boy is dead, Antonius is dead, and I killed them both. I heroically faced down Antonius and the little Pharaoh at the same time! And they both had swords - big swords! - but not bigger than mine.

SOSIUS

As you say, Caesar.

[Enter CLEOPATRA, *stage right.]*

CLEOPATRA

So this is the new Caesar?

OCTAVIAN

And this the old Cleopatra.

CLEOPATRA

It's done then?

SOSIUS

Aye, like I was telling Caesar, I killed-

OCTAVIAN

Sosius, go and wait in the kitchen. The lady and I need privacy.

[Exit SOSIUS, *stage left.]*

OCTAVIAN

It's nearly done. Antonius is dead, Caesar's bastard is dead-

CLEOPATRA

And my jewels?

OCTAVIAN

Yes, I'll need those as well of course.

CLEOPATRA

No! Lepidus gave me your word.

OCTAVIAN

I don't favor that word. You won't use it again. And Lepidus only gave you his word, but don't worry, your children by Antonius pose no threat to Rome. No harm will come to them-

CLEOPATRA

My effects are my own! You can't have my jewels!

OCTAVIAN

Can't is a cousin of no, and both are unwelcome in my presence.

CLEOPATRA

I curse the day your mother spread her legs and let you claw your way from her poisonous womb!

OCTAVIAN

That's no way to begin our trip together!

CLEOPATRA

Trip? What trip?

OCTAVIAN

You'll have to return to Rome if you want to stay near your children.

CLEOPATRA

No. My life is mine alone, and I'd sooner die than return to Rome.

[Exit CLEOPATRA, *stage right.]*

OCTAVIAN

Women - always making overblown threats that they have no intention of fulfilling. Anyway, she can't die yet - I haven't commanded it.

[Exit OCTAVIAN, *stage right.]*

ACT VI

Outside Cleopatra's Palace.

[Enter TURPIO *and* CAESARION, *center.]*

TURPIO

So, two slaves walk out of a palace in Alexandria.

CAESARION

What now?

TURPIO

Now, it's time to depart while I have a head start - before Caesar gets smart, or the plot falls apart!

[Exit TURPIO, *followed by* CAESARION,

stage right.]

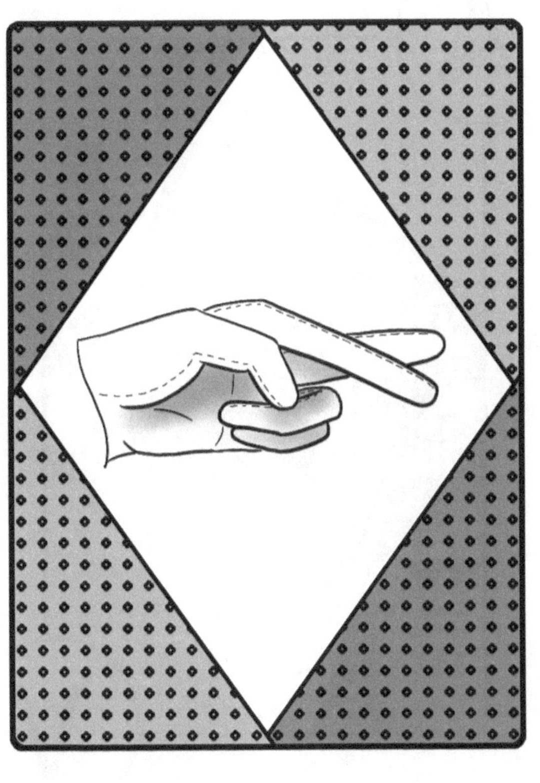

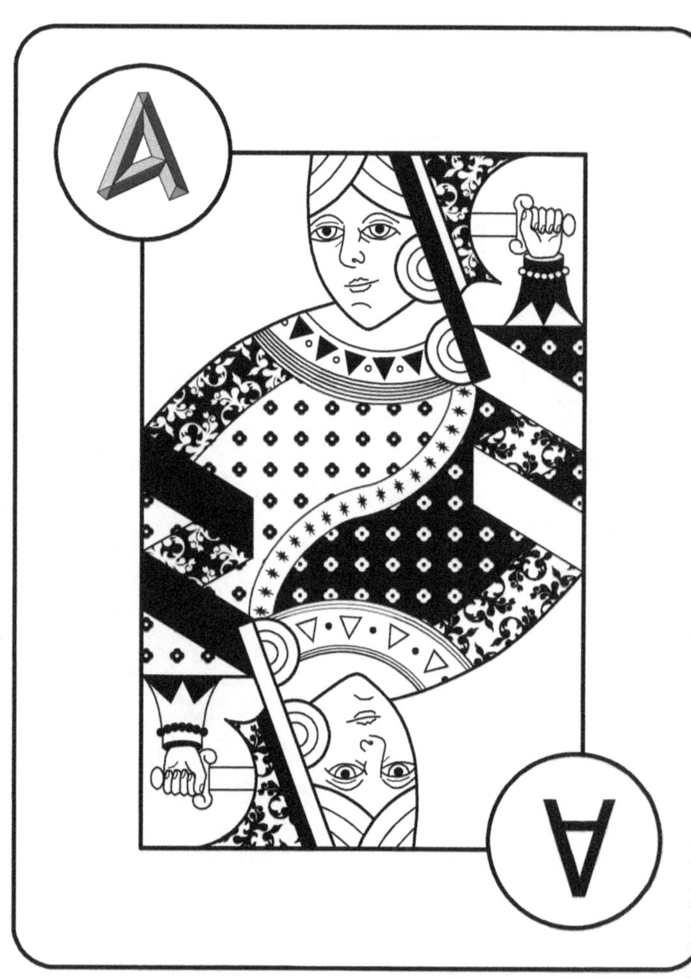

The Atlantiad

Dramatis Personae

Theodosius
King of Atlantis

Korinna
Queen of Atlantis

Sosigenes
Eldest daughter of Theodosius and Korinna

Irenaea
Youngest daughter of Theodosius and Korinna

Doulos
Slave of Theodosius

Androcles
Son of Theodosius and Korinna

Achilles
Achaea's greatest warrior, Leader of the Myrmidon army

Zeus
God of thunder, lightning, and the skies; King of Olympus

Hera
Goddess of women, marriage, and family; Queen of Olympus

Artemis
Goddess of the hunt, wilderness, and innocence

Hermes
God of trade, tricks, and thieves; Messenger of the Gods

Poseidon
God of the seas, storms, and earthquakes; King of the mortal realm

Eris
Goddess of discord

Proem

THEODOSIUS

O, you muses, fill me once more with your song. Support me so that I might tell my story and not be crushed by the weight of it. Calliope with your tablet and stylus in hand, select the words that I shall speak; inscribe them in wax and set them before my mind. Erato and Euterpe, take up your cithara and aulos and strike a tune to match my suffering - as discordant a cacophony as your Apollonian tools permit. You, Urania, spin your globe until Atlantis surfaces before you - allow your compass to point intrepid voyagers toward the place where the island once sat in the great sea. Polyhymnia behind your veil, chant and I will let the reverie of your chorus reinforce my resolve and my recollection. Terpsichore with your lyre and Thalia behind your comic mask, lend your charms to my tale and temper my despair. Clio, unfurl your endless scroll on which you have recorded every flutter of butterfly wings leading to my nadir. Finally, Melpomene, prepare your tragic mask - it will mirror what I have felt through my betrayals, and when my pain is too great I might hide my face behind it. You nine Olympian muses, aid me in telling my tale and then give my spirit rest!

[Theodosius paces across the stage.]

THEODOSIUS

Zeus, son of Kronos, to you I dedicate this story - supreme and most high ruler, you watcher of the heavens and giver of signs, you of the golden sword and the furious, boisterous orders. I thought to entrust everything to your hands, hands that couldn't be dissuaded even from snatching at your own daughter - that most serene apogee of beauty, Aphrodite. Barely was she born of the surf before you descended upon her with those hands, flawless ivory palms and long elegant fingers never betraying sinister desires. Following your own father's custom, long had you lain with your sisters before you turned your attention to your own creations. First, your daughters borne you by fellow gods, but no sooner had you created man than you decided that their daughters should not be denied you either - they too should be included in your harem of missing, mutated, and massacred wives.

[Theodosius stops pacing; centerstage.]

THEODOSIUS
One thing only remains - my story.
[*Exit* THEODOSIUS, *stage right.*]

ACT I
Scene I

The agora at Atlantis. Stage right: an apple tree marks the path to Theodosius' house. Center: a set of steps descend from the facade of a temple. Stage left: a pair of gates leads to the island's port and shore.

[Enter THEODOSIUS *and* SOSIGENES, *stage right.]*

SOSIGENES

Father, slow down!

THEODOSIUS

Quickly, Sosigenes - we must hurry.

SOSIGENES

But why? Where are we going?

THEODOSIUS

What? Nowhere.

SOSIGENES

How does one go nowhere?

THEODOSIUS

What? Don't worry, child - it's nothing.

SOSIGENES

It's not nothing. Why did you wake me so early and rush me out in such a state? Tell me.

THEODOSIUS

On account of the deathless gods. One of them came to me last night! He came as a bull wearing a crown of laurel, and he plucked a blossom from the bough of an apple tree. It was almighty Zeus himself delivering a message of salvation! He showed me how we - you and I - can ensure safety for all of Atlantis.

SOSIGENES

I thought that's why you betrothed me to god-like Achilles, sacker of cities.

THEODOSIUS

Achilles! I'll tell you his wedding offer, daughter - 'a son or a conqueror,' he said, offering me an olive branch with one hand while brandishing his spear with the other.

SOSIGENES

But, father, the gods sanctioned my marriage to swift-footed Achilles - who are we to interrupt their will?

THEODOSIUS

Yes, as you say daughter: who are we to interrupt the will of Zeus? Come, I will tell you more of my dream.

[Exit THEODOSIUS *and* SOSIGENES,

stage left.]

[Enter DOULOS, *stage right.]*

DOULOS

How many years will Doulos - wretched slave that he is - spend toiling in Atlantis? First his master sends him this way, then that, then back again - like a chained bird flittering about. Why, Fortune, do you smile always on Theodosius while you spit on Doulos? Other men suffer and triumph in equal share - their wealths and healths do wax and wane - yet never Theodosius. Ah, well, if Doulos must be a slave, best to be slave of Zeus' favorite suppliant. 'Tis better to be born a slave who enjoys the prosperity of Zeus' bounty than to be born free and suffer like Iapetos' son, who took on mighty Zeus, master of the fates of men and gods.

[Enter KORINNA *and* IRENAEA, *stage right. Korinna wears a green ribbon in her hair. Irenaea skips over to the temple and hides behind a column.]*

KORINNA

Doulos, I thought I might find you here. My husband keeps you up again? I'm afraid you must serve as our seawall, absorbing the interminable might of Poseidon's crashing waves - or is it Zeus' thunder? So much noise, and yet-

DOULOS

This one could not say, my lady - 'tis not a slave's place.

KORINNA

Well, aren't you philosophical this morning? Tell me - where is Theodosius? Where is Sosigenes? I awoke to a nearly empty house.

DOULOS

The master left with Sosigenes before this one had awoken.

KORINNA

And where have they gone, you stubborn man?

DOULOS

You might try the shore, my lady. The master has been spending much of his time there these last days. He is eager for the return of his son.

KORINNA

Androcles took his place among our fighting men at sea because such is the duty of young men of Atlantis - they must venture into the world to seize the prosperity that Zeus allots them. They grow into men of strength and character as they see the lands of distant gods and men, along with the cities and homes of our allies. Spartan mothers may claim that only they birth real men, but the sons of Atlantis grow into men capable of more than wanton butchery. Our men are poets, philosophers, orators - they can negotiate peace with words, and guarantee that peace with sword and spear only when necessary.

DOULOS

You blaspheme against the nature of the gods. They care not for Atlantis or her sons. The gods are indifferent to the lives of men.

KORINNA

That's enough, Doulos. Take your sacrilege and your anger away from this place.

DOULOS

As my lady commands.

[Exit DOULOS, *stage right.]*

KORINNA

I'll not let that old grump ruin my day - today is a day for my daughter - today Sosigenes will wed! On some lesser island she would have already been a mother by now, but we don't let our girls fall prey to lecherous abduction on Atlantis. Now, Sosigenes is ready. Irenaea will benefit from seeing what she too might achieve as a woman of Atlantis. Although, she still has plenty of time before her own marriage - time to visit nearby cities and study in the gardens of the nymphs, time to learn the tales of heroic mortals and deathless gods, time to fill her lungs with the breath of the muses. What man would not want such a learned wife as that, with whom he might discuss matters both trivial and lofty? Surely any man would prize such a wife beyond all else.

[Enter THEODOSIUS, *stage left.]*

KORINNA

There you are. I feared the worst when I awoke to an empty bed this morning. Had Zeus taken yet another son of Tros for his cupbearer?

THEODOSIUS

Oh, very funny, dearest wife.

KORINNA

Dearest wife? Have you others then? Is that why you rush off in the small hours of the morning? I think even Phaeton was yet asleep, dreaming of his father's chariot. Where is Sosigenes? I must begin preparing her for her wedding.

THEODOSIUS

Oh, she was on the shore with me. I've hardly had a minute to spend with the girl these past years, and now we will share far less.

KORINNA

So that's your ploy? You take her in secret to whisper in her ear? About what, sly one? Tell me - should Achilles have courted you instead of her?

THEODOSIUS

Enough about Sosigenes. Where is Irenaea?
Did you bring her with you? I see her not
about the agora.

[Irenaea sings out from behind a column.]

IRENAEA

Mother, mother of the bride,
    Easy to be recognized
    On Atlantis, far and wide.
Mother, mother of the bride,
    Known by all for what she wears -
    A long green ribbon in her hair!

THEODOSIUS

That's enough, Irenaea. You're too old for
childish games.

IRENAEA

Childish games? I was just playing hide and
seek with the god of this temple. She's win-
ning though - I can't seem to find her any-
where!

THEODOSIUS

Do not mock the gods, child.

IRENAEA

No, father, not I - not the daughter of
Theodosius, most reverent of all men - who
am I to question the plans of the gods?

THEODOSIUS

You know as much of the gods' plans for us as
our apples know of our plans for them.

IRENAEA

Are we then merely the food of the gods? Are
we all waiting to be sown, plucked, or reaped?

THEODOSIUS

That's enough, Irenaea.

IRENAEA

I'll go help Sosigenes prepare for her wedding
too then.

THEODOSIUS

You have no need of your sister, and your
sister has no need of you - she is a woman now
and can tend to herself.

KORINNA

Nonsense, husband. Sosigenes has need of
both Irenaea and myself, just as I had my own
mother and sisters prepare me before our
wedding.

THEODOSIUS

Sosigenes needs no preparations.

KORINNA

How can that be? Where is she?

THEODOSIUS

Listen, Korinna - the Lord of the Thundercloud came to me himself just last night.

KORINNA

Zeus came to you last night and you didn't
think to wake me?

THEODOSIUS

There was no time! You must obey when Zeus
commands!

KORINNA

Command? What command?

THEODOSIUS

The blossom-

KORINNA

What blossom?

THEODOSIUS

From the apple tree-

KORINNA

Apple tree? What are you talking about? And
what have you done with Sosigenes?

THEODOSIUS

Yes, well, you see-

KORINNA

Where is my daughter?

IRENAEA

Where's Sosigenes?

KORINNA

What have you done with my daughter?

IRENAEA

Where is she?

THEODOSIUS

I've given her to Zeus! That's what he commanded, and I obeyed.

KORINNA

You've done what? You've given my daughter away?

THEODOSIUS

To Zeus! She will be his wife, a queen, more exalted than any other!

KORINNA

And what of Achilles?

THEODOSIUS

Achilles came here - to our home - and demanded a union of our houses. He would steal my daughter with no thought of just compensation!

KORINNA

So it's about money!

THEODOSIUS

It's about safety! An alliance with Zeus will keep us safe!

KORINNA

And how will Sosigenes stay safe?

THEODOSIUS

This is why the dispassionate sex must rule. I'm guaranteeing safety for all of Olympus, not just my own family

KORINNA

Safer than an alliance with Achilles?

THEODOSIUS

A marriage to Achilles brings us an alliance with the Myrmidons. A marriage to Zeus brings us an alliance with the Olympians!

KORINNA

No, it brings only an alliance with Zeus, and even that cannot be trusted. The other Olympians will hound our daughter unto her death!

THEODOSIUS

He promised us safety! And glory for our son. Atlantis will even grow to her former stature. Don't you see? We're all saved!

IRENAEA

And Sosigenes? My sister? How is she to be saved?

THEODOSIUS

Saved from what? Don't you understand? She is to wed Zeus. She will have the most prominent marriage any woman could ask for.

KORINNA

The only marriage a woman might want less would be to you, Theodosius. Would that I had cast myself from the cliffs of Scyros that day my father gave me to you. Oh, gods, I am the most miserable of all Lycomedes' daughters!

THEODOSIUS

How can you say such a thing to me?

KORINNA

You have delivered my child unto her death - you may as well have killed her while she slept and me with her!

IRENAEA

And me!

THEODOSIUS

What is this nonsense? Who would not want Zeus as a husband?

KORINNA

His wife foremost, Hera, who has suffered his countless betrayals. But not only does Zeus offend his natural wife, he abandons his mistresses to whatever fates they should be forced to endure! They are the lost women of the Mediterranean! And what of Achilles? He will be here today, Theodosius! He is expecting to find Sosigenes ready to wed him.

THEODOSIUS

He is expecting a daughter of Atlantis - a daughter of Theodosius - nothing more.

KORINNA

What then, Irenaea? Absolutely not.

THEODOSIUS

Achilles will never know the difference.

KORINNA

Achilles is expecting a woman, not a child! And who are you to sell my children like this?

THEODOSIUS

It is not for you to say when Irenaea might marry. That decision is mine to make by the laws of gods and men.

IRENAEA

And what of the laws of women?

THEODOSIUS

It's my right, divinely prescribed by Zeus!

KORINNA

How fortunate for you that Zeus should make such pronouncements - each and every time supporting your position! And how else should it be since you are the one interpreting the declarations?

THEODOSIUS

I'll not remain to listen to this - this - this blasphemy! You will both offend our savior!

IRENAEA

And who will be Sosigenes' savior?

> *[Exit* THEODOSIUS, *stage right.]*

IRENAEA

Who will be Sosigenes' savior?

KORINNA

Savior? Surely you realize there's no saving her now - your wise and lordly father has traded her away like a sack of apples!

IRENAEA

Then who shall be her redeemer?

KORINNA

Redeemer? No, Irenaea, we mustn't think like that - this is a time for prayer and offerings. Your father was right about one thing - the will of the gods cannot be questioned by mortals.

IRENAEA

And what about my will?

KORINNA

Our protectresses will not have forgotten us. If there is a goddess among Olympus who will aid us in our quest for justice, let her hear our prayers. Surely Hera will help us, and perhaps others - Artemis, Aphrodite, Persephone, or any other of the white-armed goddesses on high. We will beseech them all. Come, Irenaea.

[Exit KORINNA*, temple.]*

IRENAEA

Bow down before those who allowed this atrocity to occur in the first place? Never - these gods of my parents will never be mine. My sister was stolen from me! If the gods truly existed, they would not have asked my father to make such a sacrosanct offering as that. Either they don't exist, or they care nothing for mortals. Whichever may be the case, it hardly matters to me now. No, the gods will not help me, so I will help myself - now is the time to do as I will. My sister is gone forever, and the gods will never receive libations from me. As for my father, he must bear the blame for the horror of my sister's fate. I swear by her name that I will raze his beloved city to the ground - this city for which he sacrifices one daughter, and then immediately offers up the other. I will see the walls crumble like ridges of sand falling into the sea. I will watch the temples burn, their altars and idols engulfed in flames. I will paint my face black with the ashes of this city and be the grim hound that haunts her even in death!

[*Exit* IRENAEA, *stage left.*]

ACT I
Scene II

[Enter ZEUS *and* SOSIGENES, *stage left.]*

SOSIGENES

Where are we? This looks just the same as the agora at Atlantis.

ZEUS

This is the agora at Atlantis, but we walk among the Olympian plane rather than that of the mortals.

SOSIGENES

How do I walk among the Olympian plane?

ZEUS

Olympians such as I can cross at will.

SOSIGENES

And I?

ZEUS

You are here because I have brought you here. Now hurry, my dear - the wedding must take place shortly.

SOSIGENES

How does Zeus know of my wedding? And where is Achilles? Should we not wait?

ZEUS

Wait? We have no time to wait.

SOSIGENES

We have to wait for the groom at least.
Achilles should be here any moment - that's
why my father brought me to the beach so
early.

ZEUS

The groom is already here, silly girl. Now,
let's get on with it.

SOSIGENES

Achilles is here? But where? Is he hiding?

ZEUS

You are not to wed Achilles. I am to be your
husband.

SOSIGENES

You - you are, my lord?

ZEUS

This displeases you?

SOSIGENES

It's only - I have always looked to you as a
protector, like my father.

ZEUS

You will learn to see me as much more than
that.

SOSIGENES

And Achilles?

ZEUS

He is of no further concern to you. You will
forget him. Now, we must finish this wedding
quickly - before the other gods arrive.

SOSIGENES

Should we not wait for them? Won't they attend the marriage?

ZEUS

Why would I want to wait for them? Should my wife watch while I wed you? And my brothers and children, what of them? Think what they would say if they sought to wed a mortal of their own - they'd say: 'Zeus did it, so too might I.' No, we do this now. Alone.

SOSIGENES

So I'm to be your secret wife? Tell me - will I be a prisoner of some high tower or an exile on some distant island?

ZEUS

You will be a wife of Zeus. Your children will be demigods, blessed beyond all other mortals.

SOSIGENES

And hated beyond all others too. The other mortals will begrudge them their gifts from jealousy while the other gods will spite them from pride. And what of Hera? Will she not hound them across the world until she sees them suffer and die?

ZEUS

And who are you to interrupt my will? We will be wed or you will fall dead. This is my decree. Come over here and lie down. Quickly, before the others arrive!

SOSIGENES

Y-y-yes, my lord. Only, wh-h-h-y are the others coming if n-n-not for a m-m-marriage?

ZEUS

They are coming for a marriage - that of Achilles and Irenaea. Now lie down!

SOSIGENES

I am to be your secret whore while Achilles marries my little sister?

ZEUS

Very well, I'll do it your way.

[Zeus grabs Sosigenes and pins her against the apple tree.]

SOSIGENES

No! Stop!

[Whistling sounds offstage.]

ZEUS

Damnit! One of the other Olympians must be approaching! I'll keep you somewhere safe for now.

[Zeus forces Sosigenes behind the tree.
When she disappears, a green apple appears on the bough.]

ZEUS

There - an apple for later.

[Exit ZEUS, stage right.]
[Enter HERMES and ARTEMIS, stage left.
Hermes whistles as he enters.]

HERMES

What boredom reigns today. I say, Artemis, give me a bit of sport - come have a duel with me! The morning is threatening to run in reverse if I don't find some amusement.

ARTEMIS

I'll not be hacking off any of your limbs today, brother.

HERMES

Just one quick stroke, I beg you! My neck is your canvas - paint with that enormous brush of yours, that sleek javelin!

ARTEMIS

Immortality doesn't suit you. Better you were born mortal - maybe a son of Daedalus?

HERMES

Ah, but at least his story lives on, while the fallen hero rests.

ARTEMIS

You've missed the point of his story if you think Icarus is the hero. And he doesn't rest brother - he's dead. He did not die well, plummeting toward Earth engulfed in flames.

HERMES

It's you who has missed the point, sister. Always so dire! Icarus may be dead, but consider how he lived. He dared to reach out and touch the stars.

ARTEMIS

Small consolation.

HERMES

Don't you see? He flew when no other mortals could!

ARTEMIS

What about the artificer himself?

HERMES

What might we gods then do if we only try? Is almighty Zeus the only one of us who might wield the lightning bolt and marshal the thundercloud? Why not us? Sometimes, sister, I feel a fire inside me, coursing through my veins like mercury! I can create - inspire love, art, and harmony; or I can destroy - raze cities, kill men, sink ships! Why should I be denied my machinations? Why should any of us? Why prostrate ourselves before Zeus? 'He of the Storm Cloud?' More like 'He of the Shepherds' Daughters!'

ARTEMIS

You ought to watch where you say such things. Those loose lips of yours are bound to sink something. Look - here comes Hera. Do you intend to enthrall her with your egalitarianism?

HERMES

No, I daresay I have a better tale with which to entertain her. Perhaps you would like to stay

and listen. I think she will be requiring your
assistance before the act is done.

ARTEMIS

What are you up to now, little Psychopompus?
Icarus' fate is too boring for you, so you crave
Prometheus' eagle?

[Enter HERA, *stage left.]*

HERA

Good morning, Artemis, Hermes. I hope I find
you both well.

HERMES

What a day! The Queen of all Olympus! I
should say you do find us well, very well now
that you've graced us with your divine
presence.

HERA

What brings you both to spectate the mortal
plane of Atlantis so early in the day?

HERMES

Should the hours of man dictate those of the
gods? Why, I know some gods who make
great use of the time mortals spend asleep.

HERA

Artemis, you come today to attend Achilles'
wedding?

HERMES

So astute, our queen! Truly does she see all.
Perhaps we ought to call her 'Fore Sight,' eh,
Artemis?

HERA

Of course you are, and rightly so.

HERMES

Sagacity, beauty, punctuality - it is little wonder that Zeus chose you for his wife.

HERA

And why are you here, Hermes? I doubt very much that Artemis requires your assistance.

ARTEMIS

What could I possibly need from him? He could neither lift my spear, nor draw my bowstring.

HERMES

You'd both be surprised by what aid I might lend here in Atlantis or even Olympus. I came here merely in the hopes of basking in your divine presence. After all, Zeus was just here, and rarely can devoted lovers like you two bear to be apart for long. I wonder what it was that he was watching though - or doing.

HERA

Zeus has much business of which I know little and you know less. It's not your place to question him.

HERMES

What? I question Zeus? Never! But, then, who do you await? You wait on Achilles?

HERA

I do not wait on him - I am not his hand-
maiden. Although I suppose I do wait for him.
He is to wed Theodosius' daughter this morn -
a lovely girl. Yes, she seems to prove that
sometimes Zeus does give with both hands.

ARTEMIS

Who knows Zeus' greatness better than Hera?

HERMES

Oh, I daresay she knows all about Zeus'
magnanimity to beautiful and pious young
girls. Why, the girl seems to prove that sometimes Zeus does take with both hands!

HERA

Enough! I can listen to no more of your snide
remarks! Go find yourself a willing audience,
or, better yet, go and amuse yourself among
the mortals - at least you'll be among your
intellectual peers!

HERMES

Your wish shall be my command, oh one true
wife of Zeus!

[Exit HERMES, *stage left.]*

HERA

The nerve of that impudent wretch!

ARTEMIS

Having seen your ire, I think he'll not bother
us further.

HERA

I certainly hope we don't have to suffer through his presence any more.

ARTEMIS

Yet I can't celebrate his absence. Who knows the trouble he'll cause when left to his own devices.

HERA

What's this? Have you seen this, Artemis?

ARTEMIS

Seen what?

HERA

The apple. I've never seen such a fine specimen. I think it's the most perfect one of the season. This must be one of Theodosius' trees.

[Enter ZEUS, stage right.]

ZEUS

My dearest wife! And daughter! So good to see you both here. What brings you to Atlantis today?

HERA

Sosigenes is to wed Achilles today - how could I miss the ceremony? How could Artemis? Is this not what brings you here as well?

ZEUS

Of course. Who should sanction the joining if not I?

HERA

Yes, no one respects the sanctity of marriage quite like you do.

ZEUS

And you, Artemis? You're obviously here for Irenaea. She'll be pleased.

ARTEMIS

Irenaea? I doubt she'll even notice my presence. She rarely visits my altar. I'm sure she will be much too preoccupied with Sosigenes to focus on anything else.

ZEUS

An impious daughter of Theodosius? I don't believe it. I've seen her sister - I know the type of girl that Theodosius produces.

ARTEMIS

Ah, but he doesn't make them all the same. No matter, we have the right one for today - Sosigenes will make an excellent wife for Achilles.

ZEUS

Yes, yes - although, it shouldn't make such a difference, should it? Which daughter, that is. Surely Irenaea will be just as worthy a wife with a bit of time. And she's the younger of the two. I think you and Hera will do Achilles a disservice, and the girls too.

HERA

What matter is it to you? Why must you con-
stantly scheme?

ZEUS

I don't scheme.

HERA

You do. Now, where is Sosigenes? I will go to
her as a woman of Atlantis and prepare her for
her marriage.

ZEUS

What a wonderful idea! Only, are you absolutely sure Achilles wouldn't prefer the younger sister? Tell me truthfully, Artemis - would
Irenaea not be the perfect bride for Achilles?

HERA

Yes, Artemis, be truthful. Don't lie to your lord
Zeus. Who knows what plans he's conceiving.

ZEUS

What would you know of my plans? Was it not
my plan that set me atop the throne of lofty
Olympus?

ARTEMIS

I thought that was your mother, Rhea of the
swaddled rock.

ZEUS

Who are you to question me?

ARTEMIS

Am I to understand that you have already decided the girls' fates? Does our say count for nothing?

ZEUS

Enough, Artemis. What difference does it make to you which woman Achilles gets? He will get one, and he's not the type of man to fuss over names.

ARTEMIS

As you command, my lord. Should someone tell the girls? Sosigenes will be dismayed to forfeit this honor.

ZEUS

Why are you so obsessed with Sosigenes?

HERA

Why are you?

ZEUS

I? Obsessed?

HERA

Where is she, Zeus?

ZEUS

Not that it should concern you, but - I accepted the girl - as an offering.

HERA

An offering?

ZEUS

Yes, an offering. It's symbolic, dearest.

ARTEMIS

But - why? Achilles has been sailing for weeks
already. Why would you do such a thing on the
day that he will arrive?

ZEUS

Enough, Artemis.

HERA

Enough for her, perhaps. I'm not done here.
Where is Sosigenes?

ZEUS

It's done, Hera. I've made my decision and
given my command.

HERA

Command? And what command is that? That
Theodosius give you his daughter? So where is
she? Where is your offering?

ZEUS

I've put her somewhere safe.

ARTEMIS

And what about Achilles?

ZEUS

He'll be thankful that I have taken her away!
Now that she has been offered the prospect of
Zeus' companionship, how could Achilles
compare?

HERA

Yes, what a tremendous lover and partner you
are. Why, just look around to see the depth and
glory of your harem!

ZEUS

I have no desire to remain here and be abused
by you.

[Exit ZEUS, *stage right.]*

HERA

You may as well have killed the girl already,
husband. You may yet get the chance to enjoy
her - a nibble perhaps - but I will not let you
keep her.

ARTEMIS

And what about Irenaea?

HERA

Irenaea? What about her? You must realize
that Zeus cares only for himself. And when is
enough enough?

ARTEMIS

Enough?

HERA

Do we not have wills of our own? Should Zeus
alone pluck the strings of fate?

ARTEMIS

I've heard that tune before.

HERA

I'll not forget about Sosigenes, nor Korinna,
nor Irenaea, nor even Achilles. I know you feel
the same, and together we will rescue our
suppliants! I can hear Korinna calling to me
now. I must comfort her with my divine
presence.

ARTEMIS

What's Zeus started? He's stolen Sosigenes, Achilles' betrothed, and now he will have Irenaea, my suppliant, take her sister's place in Achilles' bed. And what am I to do? Am I expected to join in this battle - this ridiculously contrived fight? Oh, why can't Zeus control himself! And Hera, she will inflame this situation with her wrath. But should my altar suffer due to Zeus' actions? It's not as though Irenaea visits it, yet the child is dear to me. She has the spirit of a warrior in her soul and I will stand by her now - howsoever Irenaea might benefit here, that shall be my concern. Zeus can worry about the consequences.

[Exit ARTEMIS, stage left.]

ACT II
SCENE I

[Enter KORINNA, *temple. Her dress is
lightly spattered with blood from a
sacrifice.]*

KORINNA

Down, down, down. How many times have I
walked down these same five steps? How
many times did I bring Sosigenes and Irenaea
here to make offerings when they were young?
It is a strange path today.

[Korinna collapses at the foot of the steps.]

KORINNA

Oh, gods, won't you take pity on me? Spare
me this shame and outrage! Sosigenes is gone.
What horrible fate might she yet suffer? And
now what of Irenaea? Is she to take her sister's
place in Achilles marriage bed? And what of
me? Am I to remain in Atlantis with the
betrayer, the man who sold both my daughters
on the same day? I can't stand the thought of
it! How am I to share his home - his bed? And
when he seeks to replant his seed - more
apples for the marketplace - am I to brave this
indignity too?

[Enter HERMES, *disguised as Doulos,
stage left.]*

HERMES

Knife, hatred, tools, or fury?

KORINNA

Doulos?

HERMES

Sweet Korinna, why do you weep? Will your tears bring back Sosigenes or protect Irenaea? My dear woman, you have work to do!

KORINNA

I have work to do?

HERMES

Are there not plans you should be making?

KORINNA

What do you know of my plans?

HERMES

There's no time for questions. Where will that get us? If you truly want your plan to succeed, you must dedicate your mind to the problem at hand - do not let trivialities distract you until you have completed your endeavor.

KORINNA

It's fine for a slave to say such things, you who have so little to plan. All of your concerns are handled by us.

HERMES

Do not let pride cloud your senses, Korinna. I offer you aid when none else is forthcoming.

KORINNA

And why would you help me?

HERMES

I abhor what Theodosius did - delivering Sosigenes into the hands of Zeus whose smile hides a hideous mind full of wrath and insatiable lust. That brutish, conceited-

KORINNA

Doulos.

HERMES

Incompetent, moronic-

KORINNA

Doulos!

HERMES

Who? Er, yes, what is it?

KORINNA

Do not blaspheme. I don't know whether Zeus or Theodosius is most at fault here, but let's not flaunt our contempt lest we arouse suspicion.

HERMES

Of course. Your escape will speak louder than any epithets I can hurl at those despicable, scheming, overbearing-

KORINNA

Doulos!

HERMES

What?

KORINNA

Tell me your plan, so I may judge for myself
its merits.

HERMES

As you wish. The young warrior Achilles sails
here now. He expects to find a bride when he
arrives. That much cannot be kept from the
man. Let us use that to your advantage. After
all, an alliance with Atlantis would serve
Achilles well, but there is one which might yet
serve him better.

KORINNA

With whom?

HERMES

Your father, King Lycomedes of Scyros.

KORINNA

You want me to marry Achilles?

HERMES

If he would have you. Otherwise, Irenaea.

KORINNA

No! Irenaea will not be sold off like her sister.
If Achilles won't have me, then one of my
sisters will stand in my stead.

HERMES

This can be no idle promise, lady.

KORINNA

And it won't be. Achilles shall have a daughter
of Lycomedes rather than a daughter of Theodosius. But how am I to convince Achilles to

abandon his alliance with Atlantis on the very day the deal is to be struck?

HERMES

He will need little convincing after the tongue lashing he receives from his host.

KORINNA

Theodosius will never disrespect Achilles to the man's face - he's much too cowardly for that.

HERMES

Then you must do it.

KORINNA

I? Why would Achilles listen to me?

HERMES

You must do it as Theodosius. Don his garb and affect his character. Go to the beach and welcome Achilles as I have counseled you. In his anger at Theodosius, Achilles will be quick to accept a marriage proposal from the elegant and beautiful lady of Atlantis, who will furthermore bear him a gift.

KORINNA

What gift?

HERMES

Pray to the gods, Korinna, that they might send you a symbol of their divine recognition of this course of action. An Olympian object will convince Achilles where words may fail.

KORINNA

And what of Theodosius?

HERMES

Where is your husband now?

KORINNA

Down in the orchard.

HERMES

I will see that he remains there long enough
for you to explain everything to Irenaea. When
he returns to the agora, I will arrange your
disguise.

KORINNA

How strange that man is acting today. I've
never heard him speak like that before.

*[Enter IRENAEA, her dress also bloody,
stage left.]*

KORINNA

Irenaea, good. I've just sent Doulos to keep
your treacherous father occupied, but we
haven't much time. Where have you been?
And what's happened to your clothes?

IRENAEA

I took my ewe to the shore. I walked her into
the shallows and we sat in the cool water. She
rested her head on my lap and raised her eyes
to mine. I took her by the chin and dragged a
blade across her throat. I watched her blood
run into the Great Sea and disappear.

123

KORINNA

Irenaea! You'd waste a fine sacrifice such as that when we need divine favor now more than ever?

IRENAEA

Have we not received our share of divine attention already? What more could the gods want from us? Sosigenes is already gone - am I to be next?

KORINNA

No. I'll die before I lose both my daughters on the same day.

IRENAEA

As though you have any say in the matter. Will your gods not act as they see fit, and always in their own self interest? Why should they help you? What can you offer them? Do you imagine they will starve without your burning the glistening fat and thigh bones of cows?

KORINNA

Hera has always looked after me. Consider the prosperity of our family and you will see the goddess' goodness.

IRENAEA

Hera didn't give father his orchard.

KORINNA

You have no way of knowing in what ways she has helped our family. Who are you to guess at the gods' actions?

IRENAEA

Who are you? You suppose the gods look after
you because they have brought you to this
point, but what if they have merely built you
up to watch you fall? What if they led you
here to watch you suffer - like Sosigenes, like
my lamb?

KORINNA

Do not say such things! The gods will aid us,
Irenaea. You will see the scope of their power
and the depth of their compassion.

[Exit KORINNA*, temple.]*

IRENAEA

Will nothing shake her belief? Will she
continue to recite her hymns with a mouth full
of mud, covering herself in filth at the gods'
whims? Not I. And not Sosigenes. Oh, sister,
do you remember the adventures we created
on this abominable island? We discovered lost
cities, battled against great warriors, tested our
wits before kings and queens, set sail on the
greatest seas of the world. And now how do
you suffer?

[Enter DOULOS*, stage right.]*

DOULOS

Every day it's the same - last five years - is
Doulos not his own man?

IRENAEA

Where did you come from?

DOULOS

You're not supposed to be here. You're supposed to be at home, preparing. There is much
to do, and who will be expected to do it all,
eh? Doulos, that's who.

IRENAEA

So then you had better get to it. Go about your
business and leave me to mine.

DOULOS

My business? Perhaps Doulos ought to be
readying his own daughter for her wedding.
But then, where is Doulos' wife? Where is his
home, his orchard? Your family is the only
business he has. Now, in your father's name,
come along.

IRENAEA

Then now is as good a time as any to find
some business of your own. I have matters that
require my attention, so I don't have time to
worry over your comings and goings.

DOULOS

You are like Doulos, girl - your only concerns
are those of your father. How do you think he
will react when he hears about your
willfulness, your disobedience?

IRENAEA

And who am I to obey? You? My father? Zeus,
your god of satyrs? Go then, and tell them of
my actions, but stop pestering me.

IRENAEA

I am no slave, not to any man nor god! I can make a plan just as well as Doulos, Theodosius, and Zeus. My mother will have to seek escape on her own, for I'll not be a tool for her to use either. And where is Justice in all of this? If she won't mete out her judgement, then that shall be my final task. I will avenge Sosigenes - a revenge so terrible that even the gods will weep to behold it! I will hide in the shadows and wait for Theodosius, like a spider perched on the periphery of her web. He will feel the sting of my bite, and I will drag him down into death! I will be like Zeus, like Achilles, slayer of men. I will be the firebrand that curses this city to annihilation - I will sate my rage with my father's blood!

[Enter THEODOSIUS, *stage right.]*

THEODOSIUS

Irenaea! What are you doing here? Doulos said-

IRENAEA

Do not speak to me, murderer.

THEODOSIUS

Murderer? Doulos was right to alert me to your ravings. I'll have have no more of it. You ought to be at home preparing for your wedding.

IRENAEA

Don't you mean Sosigenes' wedding?

THEODOSIUS

Sosigenes is not your concern.

IRENAEA

How dare you speak her name? Why don't you
call her what she was to you? Just another
apple for the market.

THEODOSIUS

And now what is she? Nothing less than the
wife of Zeus!

IRENAEA

And what of Hera in your daughter's grand
new life? Will she not mind sharing her
husband with a mortal?

THEODOSIUS

Don't be foolish, girl. Hera can do nothing
against the will of Zeus.

IRENAEA

You would be surprised by what a goddess, or
even a foolish girl, might accomplish against
the will of Zeus. Goodbye, Theodosius.

[Exit IRENAEA, *stage left.]*

THEODOSIUS

Why can't these women see that what's good
for the family, the city, the island is also good
for them? Will my daughters not be safe wed
to the most powerful men on Earth or
Olympus? Sosigenes will be an Olympian

queen, and Irenaea will be queen of Achilles'
kingdom. What more could they want? One
day they will see that my way is best. Until
then, I will make their decisions for them.

[Enter HERMES *as Doulos, stage right.]*

THEODOSIUS

Doulos? Why aren't you at home? Have you
prepared my vestments?

HERMES

Everything is in order.

THEODOSIUS

Good. And my wife?

HERMES

In the temple. She will be most displeased if
you don't join her.

THEODOSIUS

I'll not let fear of a woman sway me. I'm no
coward.

[Exit THEODOSIUS, *stage right.]*

HERMES

It is no cowardice to fear the havoc a woman's
wrath may wreak.

[Hermes remains on stage.]

ACT II
SCENE II

[Enter ZEUS, stage right.]

HERMES

Is that Zeus I spy? Come back to Atlantis so soon?

ZEUS

Hermes? What's that you're wearing? And where have you been? I could have used you earlier.

HERMES

Used me?

ZEUS

Yes, you always know how to distract. Hmm. Well now. Ahem. Have you business here today then?

HERMES

Business? They say there is to be a wedding - I am merely here to observe. Have you business here today then?

ZEUS

No use trying to fool you, eh? It's the girl - I must have her!

HERMES

The girl?

ZEUS

Theodosius' girl, Sosigenes.

HERMES

Sosigenes? Is she not somewhere safe by now?

ZEUS

Safe enough. Who might harm her now it's just the two of us? You see, I transformed her! I nearly had her earlier, but some Olympians interrupted us. I only just had time to hide the girl before they would have discovered us!

HERMES

And which Olympians espied you?

ZEUS

Oh, they didn't see me, and neither did I see them. As I said, I only just had time to hide the girl and escape myself. But now I have plenty of time, and you're here to help. Stand guard for me - there, at the gates. I'll finally have the girl!

HERMES

Do you mean she is here? What animal have you made her? Some kind of bird?

ZEUS

A bird? Why would I give her wings? No, no more animals. I turned her into an apple - one of Theodosius' apples.

HERMES

An apple? What are you going to do with an apple?

ZEUS

I'm going to turn her back.

HERMES

Turn her back?

ZEUS

Yes, turn her back!

HERMES

Dread majesty, Son of Cronus - what are you saying? A woman, a mere mortal, her doom sealed by you yourself? You'd set her free from all you commanded? Do as you please, Zeus - but none of the other deathless gods will ever praise you.

ZEUS

Why shouldn't they?

HERMES

What of the others then? The brides of Apollo forever in flight - Cassandra, Bolina, Daphne, Sinope, and Marpessa above all. You yourself sat in judgement of her case when she refused your son's advances; you allowed her to forsake Phoebus Apollo - morning dew fleeing the rising sun. Will you still deny to your own son that which you seek? If you return Sosigenes' form to her, all of your sons will demand you return their brides too - those daughters of rivers and streams, kings and queens. And if you comply and do this for your sons? The other gods have sons - yes, and daughters too. What will they say when they hear of what you've done?

ZEUS

Why should it matter if they hear? I am Zeus and my very words are divine decree!

HERMES

If only then it had not been you who transformed the girl. Had one of the other deathless gods changed her, then certainly you could change her back at the mere risk of incurring their wrath. However, since you changed the girl yourself, if you were to change her back you would be violating the ultimate and supreme decree of Zeus, our greatest god.

ZEUS

But I'm Zeus!

HERMES

I know who you are - you're the one whose words are divine decree. Although I suppose you should have been more careful with them then.

ZEUS

It's you who should be more careful. You and I are the only ones who know what I've done. Suppose I do turn the girl back? Suppose I do anything I like to her? What can one such as you do to obviate my will? Now move!

[Zeus shoves Hermes.]

[Enter ARTEMIS, *stage left.]*

ARTEMIS

Hello, Zeus, Hermes.

HERMES

Hello, Artemis. How good it is to see you again. Zeus was just expounding the benefits of a woman's company - how aptly they might apply their sweet words and the appeal of their form. But I must leave the two of you, much business remains.

[Exit HERMES, *stage left.]*

ARTEMIS

Your wife will be here shortly. Will you await her with me?

ZEUS

So you're upset with me too then, daughter?

ARTEMIS

I don't question your will, father, but what is to become of Irenaea? How is she to escape from this encounter without suffering?

ZEUS

Why should she suffer? Achilles is on his way to the island, is he not? She will wed him when he arrives and will never again need fear harm from anyone. Who would dare molest Achilles' woman?

ARTEMIS

Then you will look after the girl?

ZEUS

I have upheld my agreement with Theodosius thus far - I don't intend to cheat him.

ARTEMIS

No?

ZEUS

No - all the sons of Tros are dear to me. I have not forgotten their family. Assaracus had a son, Capys, who himself had two sons - Anchises he sired with Themiste, but he also had a son with Nesea, Nereid of the island. That son is Theodosius of Atlantis, grandson of Assaracus.

ARTEMIS

All the gods know of your love for the sons of Tros. My only concern is how this affects Irenaea.

ZEUS

She'll be fine. Nothing will happen to her.

ARTEMIS

Nor for her. Is she nothing more than a hostage?

ZEUS

That is for Achilles to decide as her husband. Now, I too have affairs that need tending.

[Exit ZEUS, *stage right.]*

ARTEMIS

You can come out now, brother.

[Enter HERMES, *stage left.]*

135

HERMES

What a tyrant! Don't be fooled by his circuitous talk - he cares only for himself. Neither Theodosius nor Achilles' lives would make a bit of difference weighed against another opportunity to sate his lust. Tros, Assaracus, Capys, Theodosius - he pretends they are dear to him, but they are no more than a stable of studs from which the brood mares have been culled, one by one as his fancy takes him.

ARTEMIS

The studs are not safe either - Ganymede can attest to that.

HERMES

Too true, sister. What then will you do to protect Irenaea?

ARTEMIS

What can I do? She won't heed me.

HERMES

Perhaps she will heed another.

ARTEMIS

Who? She cares nothing for the gods.

HERMES

Not even your brother, Apollo?

ARTEMIS

Not even him.

HERMES

She may not listen to shining Apollo, but Achilles will. The man is dear to the god, and

the god is dear to the man. If Irenaea won't
heed the god of truth and knowledge, then you
can at least ensure that Achilles keeps to your
plan. Otherwise the girl is doomed.

ARTEMIS

Irenaea must not suffer for Zeus' passions. I
will do as you counsel and disguise myself as
my brother, but this plan still lacks certainty.

HERMES

Perhaps another of the Olympians can help
you.

ARTEMIS

Who would risk incurring Zeus' wrath?

HERMES

His wife.

ARTEMIS

Hera? She will not aid me nor Irenaea. Even
her suppliants she looks after only so long as
they keep her altar.

HERMES

Korinna has kept her altar sacred and weighted
down with sacrifice. Hera will protect her. She
merely needs to give her favor to a marriage
between Achilles and Korinna. Korinna and
Irenaea will get their escape, and Achilles will
get a woman of Atlantis and a military alliance
with her father, albeit a different woman and
father than he was expecting.

ARTEMIS

Very well - I will beseech Hera to aid Korinna and thus to protect Irenaea.

HERMES

You are only doing as you must - Zeus has left you no other choice.

[Exit HERMES, *stage left.]*

ARTEMIS

Yes, I see no other way to save Irenaea, trapped on Atlantis like a fly amidst a great, shimmering spider's web. And who else but Zeus might play the role of the spider, weaving hither and thither, leaving a sticky trap behind? None are safe from his desirous eyes! That hawkish gaze of his - perennially casting about in search of some new prey - there is no hiding from it! Yet I can still ensure that no harm befalls Irenaea. I will not let her be taken like her sister. And what of Hera? How can she let Zeus carouse like this?

[Enter HERA, *temple.]*

HERA

You seek to blame me for Zeus' outrages?

ARTEMIS

Hera, whence did you arrive?

HERA

I have been sequestered in the temple for the better part of the day, and I exit to hear you

claim I am the cause of this new disgrace. I am
the victim!

ARTEMIS

Sosigenes is the victim, and Irenaea may yet
be as well.

HERA

You think I don't know that?

ARTEMIS

How then will you aid them?

HERA

Sosigenes is already doomed. It's just a matter
of time until Zeus grows bored with the girl
and lets down his defenses. Then I will find
her. But it was Zeus who stole the girl - he
created this situation! Any harm that befalls
her now is his own doing.

ARTEMIS

And Irenaea, your suppliant's child?

HERA

What is she to me?

ARTEMIS

Do you think Korinna will abandon her? What
mother would do such a thing?

HERA

Careful, daughter of Zeus.

ARTEMIS

It is Korinna and Irenaea who must now be
careful. How will you aid them in their
escape?

HERA

I? How will you?

ARTEMIS

I have a plan - a plan for Korinna and Irenaea to sail away from Atlantis.

HERA

What's this plan?

ARTEMIS

Irenaea will not wed Achilles. Instead, Korinna will wed him, and both mother and daughter will escape the island aboard Achilles sleek, black ships.

HERA

Why would Achilles agree to this plan?

ARTEMIS

He is a warrior. You must appeal to him as such. He will forsake an alliance with Atlantis for one with Korinna's father on Scyros.

HERA

He will not. Achilles is a man besides a warrior, and men always need something to sweeten their fare.

ARTEMIS

Then I will make a different plan. I will do whatever I must to protect my suppliant.

HERA

No. You will stay away from this island. Do you hear me, Artemis? Keep yourself away from Atlantis the rest of this day.

ARTEMIS

Will you keep all of Zeus' children at bay?

> *[Exit* ARTEMIS, *stage left.]*

HERA

These daughters of Zeus are infuriating! I am his rightful wife by all the laws of Olympus, and still they seek always to aid him sneak around in the shadows. They play a dangerous game. Have they forgotten about Echo? Echo, who plotted to help you, son of Kronos. Well did she know of your proclivities among the Oreads - all of Olympus knows your weakness for nymphs. The girl was clever to distract me with her amusing stories while you dallied. It was the last clever thing she ever did.

> *[Enter* HERMES, *stage left.]*

HERA

I thought we had finished with you already.

HERMES

Not quite, but why does the Queen of Olympus still brood on Atlantis?

HERA

Because my illustrious husband has forsaken me for an apple monger's daughter.

HERMES

It's hardly the first time.

HERA

A curse on your altar, Hermes!

HERMES

Why do you curse me, Hera? It is Zeus who wrongs you, not I.

HERA

And who is running about between the scenes, pulling strings and tipping blocks? Who is helping Zeus hide that wretched girl? I've been watching you, Hermes - the way you come and go.

HERMES

Do I do it so differently from the rest?

HERA

The rest may not knows your tricks, but I do.

HERMES

I have no need of tricks, but Korinna and Irenaea will need one from Achilles if they are to escape the island.

HERA

So that's your true purpose here? Artemis has sent you to argue for her plan?

HERMES

What matter whose plan if it's a good one?

HERA

I'd be inclined to agree with you if it was a good plan.

HERMES

What's wrong with it?

HERA

Have you not heard Irenaea? She's been raving quite openly about murdering her father and burning the city to the ground.

HERMES

We've all heard her ravings, but what can a young girl who has never held sword nor spear do to harm Theodosius, favorite of Zeus? The girl is merely upset. She will do as her mother bids her.

HERA

Perhaps you have a point. She is just a young girl - how much harm could she cause? And her mother has been a loyal suppliant of mine all her life. Very well, I will enlist Achilles in my plot and ensure he brings Korinna to safety, lest my altar suffers. But how to entice the man?

HERMES

A wedding gift from the Queen of Olympus should do the trick.

HERA

What kind of gift?

HERMES

It could be anything. Just apply some of your magic, give it the appeal of gold, and any object will aptly convey your intention.

[Exit HERMES, *stage left.]*

HERA

Anything, you say? Well, why not an apple? One of Theodosius' apples! I rather like the sound of that. And if Zeus can steal from Theodosius' orchard, then why mightn't I? Achilles shall have a golden apple!

[Hera plucks the apple, Sosigenes, from the bough of the apple tree.]

HERA

Ah, here's a ploy worthy even of Daedalus. Would that I had a servant such as you to build me a labyrinth or some other ingenious trap. Instead, Achilles will be my man. To think, a warrior who strikes fear into the hearts of men should be bought so cheaply. Yet why should I forever be the one to bear the cost of Zeus' games? Why do his brothers not reign him in? Can they be so satisfied with the drawing of lots? Where is Poseidon, who looks after the ships and sailors of Atlantis? Does neither this island nor its citizens concern him any longer? He too has a suppliant near.

[Exit HERA, *temple.]*

ACT III
Scene I

[Enter KORINNA, *temple. She carries the Golden Apple.]*

KORINNA

What a vision! If Hera sent the same dream to Achilles, he will certainly aid my cause. And no one will doubt the divinity of my plan when they see the goddess' gift - a solid gold apple! Even Irenaea will be convinced when I show her this.

[Exit KORINNA, *stage left.]*

[Enter THEODOSIUS, *stage right.]*

THEODOSIUS

Zeus, heavenly father, my offering has been made - Sosigenes sits by your side on Olympus. Now is the time to make good on your promises. Let the people of Atlantis see your will be done! What's this? Why is the agora not prepared for the wedding?

[Enter ANDROCLES, *stage right. He carries a javelin and wears a sword belt with a sheathed sword.]*

ANDROCLES

Did I hear there is to be a wedding?

THEODOSIUS

Yes, yes, my daughter - Androcles! Zeus be praised, you're here!

ANDROCLES

Father!

[Theodosius and Androcles embrace.]

THEODOSIUS

Come, my son, let me take a look at you. You know, I can still picture the day you left.

ANDROCLES

Has five years passed so quickly?

THEODOSIUS

Five years and still I remember as though it were yesterday. Those mighty triremes sailing under the green flags of Atlantis, they rowed all the way around the island in salute before turning to their course. Oh, what a beautiful thing to behold! But now, you are returned, and for the sight of you, I would forego all others!

ANDROCLES

You honor me, father. And my brother-to-be has arrived as well.

THEODOSIUS

He is here already?

ANDROCLES

His sleek, black ships clog the entire harbor.

THEODOSIUS

Were you able to dock?

ANDROCLES

Come, father - I am a son of Atlantis. I know the shores of this island as a clam knows the inside of its shell. My ship is just off the coast. I swam to the cliffs and scaled them like I did as a child. The house was deserted, so I thought to head to the agora. Where is the rest of the family - mother and my sisters?

THEODOSIUS

Oh, they must be preparing for the wedding with their retinue of friends - you know how women are. You'll see them all soon enough. First we must give thanks! Here, in the temple, we will thank Zeus for returning you to Atlantis.

[Androcles sets his sword and javelin down before the temple steps.]

[Exit ANDROCLES *and* THEODOSIUS, *temple.]*

[Enter KORINNA *and* IRENAEA, *stage left.]*

KORINNA

Irenaea, wait! You must hear of the vision that Hera has sent me.

IRENAEA

A vision? Really, mother, do you have any idea how ridiculous you sound?

KORINNA

See for yourself!

*[Korinna proffers the Golden Apple to
Irenaea.]*

IRENAEA

That?

KORINNA

It is our salvation!

IRENAEA

An unripened apple?

KORINNA

Unripened? It's gold, inside and out! Hera has
shown me this and other things. She has sent
me a plan - a way to escape!

IRENAEA

You are a fool if you still think the gods care
for your problems. But go on, tell me your
plan. How are you going to escape this pit of
wretchedness?

KORINNA

I will wed Achilles.

IRENAEA

You will?

KORINNA

I will, and he will take us from here. We will
go far from this island and the grasp of your
father.

IRENAEA

I do not fear my father's grasp, and I will not
run with you, mother, nor with Achilles.

KORINNA

But this is the only way I know to save you!

IRENAEA

I never asked you to save me! I will look after my own fate, and you would do best to look after your own.

KORINNA

My fate is nothing without you. I know you're angry, Irenaea, but you must be ready to leave when Achilles arrives. It is the only way.

[Exit KORINNA*, stage right.]*

IRENAEA

Still she remains loyal to her gods of filth and betrayal! I'll not participate in her absurd plot - I already have plans of my own. She may look after herself. Maybe her trinkets will be enough to secure her passage aboard Achilles' ship. That, then, is her chance for escape. Either way, her blood will not be on my hands. Oh, city of barbarians, city of false oaths, city of curses! Soon you will be a city of tombs.

[Irenaea retrieves Androcles' sword before the temple steps.]

IRENAEA

What's this? Father's sword? It can't be, but it bears the apple blossom markings of his house. When was the last time he took this down? He must have spent all day cleaning the blade to restore its luster, fool that he is! Now

149

it will be his undoing. That noise! Theodosius
must be on his way to meet Achilles.

> [Exit IRENAEA, *stage left.*]
> [Enter KORINNA, *disguised as Theodosius,*
> *stage right.*]

KORINNA

Oh, what a wretch I feel in this garb. Where
has Irenaea gone to now? We don't have time
for this - we have to get down to the beach.
Perhaps she has already made her way down
there.

> [Exit KORINNA, *stage left.*]
> [*A scream pierces the silence.*]
> [Enter IRENAEA, *stage left.*]

IRENAEA

You are avenged! Do you hear me, sister?
Theodosius is dead! Failed father and false
prophet - he is fallen. At last, he is truly dead!
And what kind of man screams so like a
woman? I had to slit his throat just to stop that
wailing. And the blood - so much blood. How
can a man with no heart have so much blood?
He was never a man at all. Oh, but that blood -
how it stains my hands. Is he truly dead? Can
it be? I will go and look upon his face once
more.

> [Exit IRENAEA, *stage left.*]
> [Enter THEODOSIUS *and* ANDROCLES,
> *stage right.*]

THEODOSIUS

That is how you court the favor of Zeus, King of Olympus, master of the fates, and commander of the deathless gods!

ANDROCLES

Well done, father. Now, let us offer a prayer to Poseidon.

THEODOSIUS

Poseidon? He may look after you at sea, but you are back in Atlantis where Zeus reigns supreme.

ANDROCLES

Steady, father - we worshiped Zeus first, but we mustn't neglect the other gods.

THEODOSIUS

You mean the lesser gods, for none can compare with the might of Zeus. If those other gods have obligations here, then Zeus will see that they are performed in accordance with divine law. I do not beg their favor - I ask only for that of Zeus.

ANDROCLES

I know you mean well, father, but you are just as stubborn and implacable as ever. Very well. In honor of your wishes, Zeus will suffice for today.

THEODOSIUS

Ah, patronizing child, you will see my way is right - you will see how Zeus rewards his suppliants.

[Enter IRENAEA, stage left. She holds Androcles' sword in one hand, and a golden apple with a piece of bloodied, green ribbon wrapped around its stem in the other.]

THEODOSIUS

Who is that man? What has he got in his hands?

ANDROCLES

A green ribbon?

IRENAEA

A green ribbon - a green ribbon from Korinna's hair. Mother, mother of the bride-

THEODOSIUS

Korinna? My Korinna?

[Androcles brandishes his spear, charges toward Irenaea, and impales her upon it. Irenaea drops the apple and clings to her brother, sword still in her hand.]

IRENAEA

Androcles?

[Androcles recoils from the blade slicing his back.]

THEODOSIUS

Kill him! Kill that man who has murdered my wife, your mother!

THEODOSIUS

How can this be? We were finally safe - she
and the rest of Atlantis - safe from any threat
from abroad! Who was that man and why
would he kill Korinna of all people?

[Enter ACHILLES, stage left.]

ACHILLES

This is how you greet your son?

THEODOSIUS

Achilles? My son?

ACHILLES

Not now that you sent a warrior with spear in
hand to attack me!

THEODOSIUS

My son - my Androcles - attack you?

ACHILLES

Great-hearted Androcles? You sent your own
son out to kill me?

THEODOSIUS

No, you fool! He was not coming after you!
He was attacking the man who murdered his
mother!

ACHILLES

What trick is this? There was no other man out
there - only a girl clutching a bit of ribbon. I
arrived just in time to see that warrior strike
her down, who can be none other than Irenaea.

153

THEODOSIUS

Irenaea? Why would she be on the beach? This
is all a mistake.

ACHILLES

It is no mistake. The girl carried the very sign
that Hera promised.

*[Achilles proffers the Golden Apple to
Theodosius.]*

THEODOSIUS

Keep that accursed thing away from me! It's
wrong - it's all wrong! The gods ordained this
alliance. How has it gone wrong?

ACHILLES

The only reason for an alliance with Atlantis
was Androcles' sword, and I would have had
that when I took his mother to my bed. Now
that both are dead, I have no need of a
deceitful coward like you.

THEODOSIUS

Stay back, Achilles! Zeus will not allow you to
kill me - not after all I've done for him, all
I've sacrificed!

ACHILLES

Zeus does not care for you. He cares for no
one but himself. Whatever you have done for
him, whatever you have sacrificed, he will not
save you.

*[Achilles kicks Theodosius over, mounts his
helpless body, and cuts out his eyes.]*

ACHILLES

Suffer what Zeus has sent you, old man, and remember that he does not give happiness unwed to despair to mere mortals - every joy is tempered with grief. I know this well myself. You were forced to watch me kill your son, but I was forced to watch him wrench my own prize from my grasp - the deliverer of your misery suffers himself. Your life, at least, he has let you keep.

[Theodosius pushes himself into a seated position against the tree.]

THEODOSIUS

Achilles! Now is your time of glory - victory is yours. A gift of the son of Cronus, Zeus. He brought Androcles down with deathless ease. If twenty Myrmidons had charged against my son, they'd all have died here, laid low by his spear. No, deadly fate killed him, and from the ranks of men, Irenaea. You came third, and all you could do was finish off his life. One more thing - take it to heart, I urge you - you too won't live long, I swear. Already I see them looming up beside you - Death and the strong force of Fate, to bring you down at the hands of Priam's great royal son. Yes, you are in their grip already. Yet, Priam's son cannot claim the glory all for his own, for one of my own children will yet have their say in the matter.

ACHILLES

You truly are a fool, Theodosius. You have no children left to you.

THEODOSIUS

You will see all when the judge takes up his bow.

[Theodosius falls back to the ground, unconscious.]

[Exit ACHILLES, *stage left.]*

[Enter DOULOS, *stage right.]*

DOULOS

There's one task done, anyway - your clothes are ready, master. Master! What's happened to him? His face, oh that lordly and majestic face now covered in blood. His eyes - where are his eyes? Useless. Where are your gods now, master? Well, no life is left for Doulos on Atlantis, and no ship awaits him in the port. He must make for Androcles' ship where he saw it at anchor. Those men know Theodosius - they will allow both aboard, and so shall Theodosius finally serve Doulos. See if those gods will help Doulos carry Theodosius past the orchard, over the cliffs, and through the water. Up now, son of Capys, and take your last look at Atlantis!

[Exit DOULOS *bearing* THEODOSIUS,

stage right.]

156

ACT III
Scene II

[Enter HERA, *temple.]*
HERA

Fool Irenaea! You've ruined it all, idiot girl! What's this? My gift, accursed thing, worthless now. Let it rest in the dust - I'll not sully my hands to touch it again. And what of Korinna? Where will be her resting place? I must go look upon her corpse at least.

[Exit HERA, *stage left.]*
[Enter ZEUS, *stage right.]*
ZEUS

At last - an empty agora. Finally, I will enjoy the fruit of my labor!

[Zeus searches the apple tree for Sosigenes.]
ZEUS

Where is she? What's this? My apple - my Sosigenes - shorn from your branch and left in the dust? Now the girl is dead for sure - she only remained alive so long as the apple remained on the branch. Who has subverted my will and wrought such horrors on this place? It can only have been Hera. Damn me for hiding the girl in plain sight! Oh, unhappy Fortune, even me you tease! Sosigenes was the fairest maiden of them all - anyone asked to judge her beauty would say the same!

[Enter HERA, *stage left.]*

HERA

So this is what comes of the best laid plans of Zeus - the annihilation of an entire family? I thought the sons of Tros were dear to you - although the daughters clearly weren't. I saw what became of Korinna, what became of Irenaea. And what of Sosigenes, husband? Has she too met her end, the poor girl? All that blood on your hands.

ZEUS

My hands? What have I to do with it? I promised Theodosius Achilles, and Achilles came. How am I to account for your deceit, your treachery? You are more at fault than anyone for the blood spilled here today!

HERA

You seek to lay those corpses at my feet?

ZEUS

You may lay their corpses wherever you like, along with your blame, but I'll not mourn those lifeless bodies lying in the surf. Does the sand mourn them? Does the ocean? Then why would I, who am deathless too? Why would you?

HERA

So I should reserve myself to inaction while you steal the daughters of my suppliants? Those girls have two parents. Whatever arrangements you make with the fathers, the mothers come to me. They flock to my altar. They ask me why they must bear such punishments.

ZEUS

They're just humans! It matters little which of them dies or which of them lies with me.

HERA

And you're just an Olympian, one of many!

[Exit HERA, *temple.]*

ZEUS

Irrational woman! Do I complain when she curses and tortures my mortal children? And when she kills them, do I drag their corpses to her altar? It's absurd! They're just humans, after all.

[Enter POSEIDON *and* ARTEMIS,
disguised as Apollo, stage left.]

POSEIDON

Brother, what has happened here? How come I to pass the expired body of Androcles, my suppliant?

ZEUS

Poseidon? You too seek to meddle in my affairs on Atlantis?

159

POSEIDON

Meddle? What concern is it of mine what affairs you conduct, here or elsewhere? I only ask about my suppliant.

ZEUS

And you, Apollo? What have you to say? What thin excuse brings you here of all places on today of all days?

POSEIDON

Do not ignore me, brother! What has happened to Androcles?

ZEUS

Ah, now it's clear - you both had a hand in this! This is no coincidence - it's a plot! An insurrection! Does this little coterie seek to dethrone me? You, Poseidon, you wish to redraw the lots? You wish to wield the flaming thundercloud? What would you have me do, brother? Answer me!

POSEIDON

There is no satisfactory answer that I can provide you. You have already made up your mind.

ZEUS

And you, Apollo? I take your silence as acknowledgement of your guilt, alongside Poseidon, in this absurd plan of Hera's, this failed rebellion! I curse you both! I cast you out - from the time the sun sets today, you both

shall walk the mortal plane as exiles of Mount
Olympus! Your disgrace will end when you
have spent a full mortal year in servitude -
only then will this insult have been repaid.

[*Exit* ZEUS, *stage right.*]

POSEIDON

One of my dearest suppliants has been
murdered most treacherously, and now I'm
cursed by Zeus and exiled from Olympus -
how comes this to pass, Phoebus? Nay, stay
your explanation. There is no profit to be had
from wondering at such terrible knowledge.
Zeus has made his declaration and now we
must suffer, rightly or otherwise. For myself,
there is only one mortal of which I know who
deserves my divine aid - Laomedon, son of
Ilus. He is building a wondrous city in the
East. That is where I shall go.

[*Enter* HERA, *temple.*]

ARTEMIS

Look upon the cost of your proclamations,
Queen of Olympus!

HERA

Artemis? You dare to defy my commands?

ARTEMIS

To save my suppliants, I would defy you
across every realm of existence.

HERA

To what end? You have defied me - have you saved your suppliant?

ARTEMIS

That was more your fault than mine!

HERA

My fault? You are as dramatic and idealistic as ever.

ARTEMIS

And your sycophancy is only rivaled by your apathy! You too have a dead suppliant out there on the beach, her lifeblood leaking into the ocean. What did you do to save her?

HERA

Yours lies there too, daughter of Zeus, despite all your plans.

ARTEMIS

What would you have me do then?

HERA

Abide by the laws of Olympus!

ARTEMIS

The same ones that justify Zeus' actions? I would rather abide by the laws of right than might. Uncle, if you go to Laomedon at Troy, my brother will go there too. Misery is better endured with companionship.

POSEIDON

Yes, if serve we must, then let us serve in the
furtherance of true greatness. Let us see what
we can make of this Troy.

HERA

You would bestow such privilege on Ilium?
Why not Athens-

POSEIDON

You know why I won't serve the Athenians!

HERA

What about Argos, Samos, or Sparta?

POSEIDON

Those are yours to guard, yours to improve.

ARTEMIS

I too will go to Troy.

HERA

You will?

ARTEMIS

That is, Apollo will go to Troy, but I will not
be far off - ever at hand should my brother
need me, ever ready to remind him why he
suffers.

[Exit ARTEMIS, *stage left.]*

HERA

Oh, a curse on the house of Tros! A curse on
the sons of Ilus and Assaracus, Laomedon and
Capys! Would that I could send them a gift -
Ganymede with his throat slit and his lifeblood

emptied into the very goblet he has borne for Zeus!

[Enter HERMES, *stage left.]*

HERMES

Just dump him on the beach when you do kill him - it's a mess out there already.

HERA

I'm not murdering Ganymede! I'm just trying to make a point - do you see the power that Zeus wields with such carelessness?

POSEIDON

Power which you might better wield?

HERA

The Olympians would never suffer a woman to rule them. No, I can never brandish the flaming thundercloud.

POSEIDON

Tell me - who then?

HERMES

Yes, my queen, tell us!

HERA

There are two of whom I can think who might sit atop the Olympian throne. You know of whom I speak, brother.

POSEIDON

You seek fruit from a barren tree, sister. The lots were fairly drawn, and I do not lust after my brothers' kingdoms nor their power. Zeus holds what is above, all that lies within the watery depths is mine, and everything below belongs to Hades. And while our kingdoms may lie below that of Zeus, they are not inferior, and neither are we. There, in the seas, I am the powerful one. It is I who wields the Silver Trident - I am the one who commands and controls all. You haven't the vaguest notion of the intrigues and occurrences of my court. Think then what you might know of Hades' kingdom, which lies beyond even the deepest reaches of my own - Hades whose gleaming helm permits him to travel unseen throughout all the realms, who guards his charges and his kingdom more voraciously than any other. Yet I do not look with jealousy at Hades nor at Zeus nor even at their consorts.

HERA

And what of your suppliants here in Zeus' realm? I saw one of yours out there in the sand. Tell me, what was his name?

POSEIDON

Androcles.

HERA

A fine name.

HERMES

Any name suits a corpse fine. What difference now what you call him?

POSEIDON

He was a fine man - honorable, pious, and the greatest warrior of all my suppliants.

HERA

He was the greatest warrior of all mortals! Only this young Achilles could defeat him, and not without the help of Zeus' ruse. But which other of our suppliants might Zeus decide to take? How will you stop him when he comes for one of your own? This task falls to the two of us.

HERMES

Three of us.

HERA

Very well, the three of us. We must swear a pact of allegiance to one another.

POSEIDON

A pact?

HERA

A pact.

POSEIDON

As you wish, sister.

[Hera, Hermes, and Poseidon stand in a circle with clasped hands.]

HERA

To resist and oppose Zeus' will. To guard over the cities which are sacred to us each-

POSEIDON

To protect our suppliants.

HERA

To protect our suppliants and guide them to glory-

POSEIDON

Guide them to safety.

HERA

To see our altars piled high with sacrifice-

HERMES

To allay banality, ennui, and malaise.

POSEIDON

Let the pact be sworn then. I have little time left before I depart for Ilium.

HERA

You go to Ilium in the company of Apollo, whose sister is recently determined to oppose me? You violate our accord even before the words have finished being spoken!

POSEIDON

Our accord concerns Zeus. You'll not set me at odds with all the gods of Olympus - my brothers and sisters, nieces and nephews. I go to Ilium to serve my term of punishment, one which I have done nothing to deserve.

HERA

Yet we all know who is at fault for such an outcome!

[Exit HERA, *stage left.]*

POSEIDON

You and I both know that Zeus did not cause all that has occurred here today.

HERMES

Of course not. Hera and Artemis played their own roles also.

POSEIDON

And who, I wonder, choreographed their movements?

HERMES

They are deathless gods, two of the most powerful among us. I doubt very much whether any god could have so influenced them.

POSEIDON

Indeed. Which of the gods has such power? Perhaps we should look to the messenger.

HERMES

What could a simple messenger do to create such havoc as ensued today?

POSEIDON

That I hope never to discover. If I did, Androcles' death would require justice.

[Hermes begins to whistle.]

POSEIDON

Am I boring you, nephew? Go then and bring no further despair to this place.

[Exit HERMES, *stage left.]*

POSEIDON

Behold Atlantis - behold the souls of those who anger overcame. Some god knows the unholy deceit that has brought this island low, while the rest of us might only guess. And will the assigning of blame bring back the dead? There is one thing at least that I can do for this wretched island. I call to my subjects in every corner of my realm. I call on you all to listen to my words and see my will enacted, to cause the sea to rise and the earth to tremble, to take this island, forsaken by her gods. Take her gates, her temple, her orchard. Give them all to the sea. Take this barren tree and petrify it - let the thing sink and turn to stone. Most of all, take this accursed apple, foul and unholy as it is - take it to the bottom of the sea and there finally give calm to a tortured and wretched being.

[Exit POSEIDON, *stage left.]*

[Enter ERIS, *temple.]*

ERIS

Hear me now, you deathless gods. Another is come - another swells your ranks - I, who was formerly mortal but have been smiled upon by some power beyond even treacherous Zeus' control. Yes, I was a mortal born of mortal parents with famous names. I cast them aside with my own, cast them aside to the void from which I come. Born in blood and baptized in darkness, I emerge anew - Eris, daughter of night and bringer of discord!

[Eris retrieves the Golden Apple.]

ERIS

Come with me, sister, away from this sinking place.

[Exit ERIS, *stage right.]*

ACT IV
Scene I

THEODOSIUS

Now you know my tragedy, or rather how it begins. You too know how my wrathful family tore itself apart like a many headed wolf,- snarling and snapping at its own belly, chomping down on hunks of flesh and rending them from its body - until nothing was left but a bloody mess amid bodiless heads. In such a way, the gods took my family from me. But now I must stop - I must not tell of further misery. Already every star is falling that was ascending when I began my tale, and to stay too long is not permitted.

[Exit THEODOSIUS, *stage left.]*

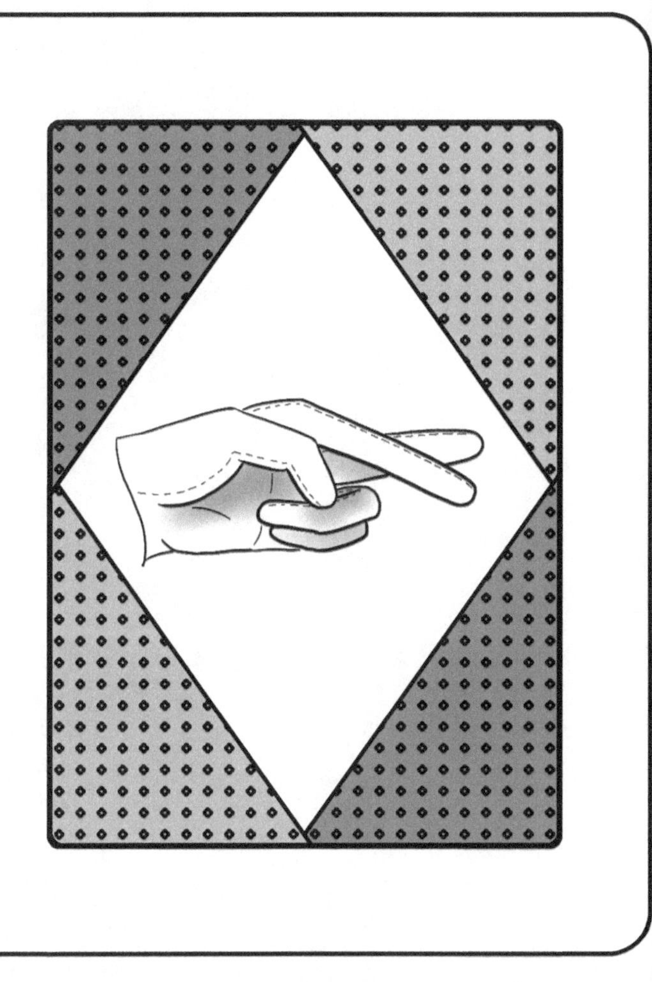

About the author

John Carney is a writer from Jupiter,
Florida. After serving in the military, he
went to college and became a teacher.